SHUTTERspeed
a SNAPshot novella

by

FREYA BARKER

Shutter Speed
a novella

Copyright © 2016 Margreet Asselbergs as Freya Barker

All rights reserved.

No part of this publication may be reproduced, distributed, or transmitted in any form or by any means, including photocopying, recording, or by other electronic or mechanical methods, without the prior written permission of the author or publisher, except in the case of brief quotations embodied in used critical reviews and certain other non-commercial uses as permitted by copyright law. For permission requests, write to the author, mentioning in the subject line:
"Reproduction Request" at the address below:
freyabarker.writes@gmail.com

This book is a work of fiction and any resemblance to any person or persons, living or dead, any event, occurrence, or incident is purely coincidental. The characters and story lines are created and thought up from the author's imagination or are used fictitiously.

ISBN: 978-1-988733-00-5

Cover Design:
RE&D - Margreet Asselbergs
Editing:
Karen Hrdlicka

DEDICATION

For my amazing readers!!

I appreciate each and every one of you. Thank you for allowing me to do what I love to do so much!

BLURB

She likes picking up her camera because it allows her to see things through a different lens. Like when she lost her job recently and instead of focusing on what she's forced to leave behind, she zooms in on the new options opening up in front of her. Or when a dangerous looking silver fox comes rolling up her path on a FatBoy, and her digital output shows a deep loneliness, matching her own, in his ice-blue eyes.

But when she's working on making her dreams come true, she inadvertently captures something in her viewfinder she can't un-see.

He wasn't supposed to be here, but he can't seem to escape his old life. Stuck in an old trailer in the mountains, he walks a fine line between ruse and reality. With the arrival of a young-looking pixie—who turns out to be a full grown, hot-blooded woman—his balance is thrown.

He tries to avoid her, but with the little pixel peeper snapping everything in sight, she unintentionally risks his exposure.

And his focus needs to be sharp to keep her from danger.

CHAPTER I

"Are you gonna be all right?"

My uncle Al is stuffing the last of his bags in the trunk of his old Cadillac DeVille. He's had that car since he retired almost twenty years ago, and I have some fond memories in the backseat of that boat. My black Beetle looks ridiculously small parked next to it, but at least it's economical.

"I'll be fine," I assure him again. "Besides, if I have questions or run into trouble, I can always call."

"Just make sure to empty the bins every night," he reminds me, concern marking his face. "There've been some bear sightings up on the mountain, and as much as most campers get excited about it, they'd still prefer not to find one on their campground."

"Good thing you left behind a whole box of shotgun shells then, right? Don't worry," I hurry to promise. "I'll practice loading and shooting today." Uncle Al rolls his eyes up to the heavens.

"Just don't shoot any campers, please," he begs.

"Just with my camera," I quip before turning serious. "Look, I don't want you to worry about anything, okay? You just take care of getting Ginnie settled in."

My uncle's second wife has Alzheimer's. The decline has sped up in the past few months, but my uncle had hoped to be able to finish out the summer here. Ever since he took early retirement from the police force at fifty-five, they'd come up to McPhee Reservoir and looked after one of the campgrounds during the summer season. They have a big trailer with all the amenities hauled up the mountain in early May of each year, which they need, because other than water and electrical hookups, the campground doesn't have much on offer. A few outhouses in strategic places and a bathhouse with two shower stalls are about the extent of it. Oh, and an old-fashioned phone booth, something I don't consider a luxury since cell phone reception is spotty at best here.

Unfortunately, only three weeks into their stay, and already Ginnie had wandered off a handful of times. Uncle Al had to call in the help of some early season campers to find her. The last time she ended up to her waist in the reservoir, not knowing how she got there. That was the last straw. He drove her back home to Flagstaff, called me, and offered me the most exciting opportunity I've had in forever.

It took me only a day to pull up stakes and one more to drive here from Glenwood Springs. Uncle Al had left his wife in the care of a trusted neighbor, for a few days, and was waiting for me when I pulled in. Yesterday, he took me around the grounds in his golf cart, showing me the ropes, and today he's heading back.

His big burly arms tightly wrap around me in a hug. Still one of the best huggers I know, my uncle. The first time I realized that was the day we buried my mom, his younger sister. I'd been twelve at the time and had never felt the lack of a father more than in that moment. He just wrapped me up against his barrel chest. In that moment, I felt safer than ever before. Mom had been a single mother, and I didn't even know who my father had been. Apparently neither did she. My uncle and aunt, who didn't have kids of their own, took me in. Despite the fact I was hell on wheels as a teenager, they loved me to distraction. I was heartbroken when Aunt Kate died only five years later from a massive aneurism. I'd been seventeen. It had been just him and me for a few years then and we looked after each other. Then Uncle Al met Ginnie and I'd started feeling like a fifth wheel. Within a year, I moved away, determined to find my own place in the world. The grand total left of my family was Uncle Al, and I'd already depended on him for too long. I'd been twenty-two, that was seventeen years ago. Nestled against his familiar chest, his arms banding around me, it's like time never passed. I'm still that scared twelve-year-old, afraid to face the world alone.

Swallowing hard to stave off the threatening tears, I slowly pull from his hold.

"Are you sure?" he asks again, his sharp gaze not missing the watery state of my eyes.

"I promise," I say with much more confidence than I feel.

"Just remember, the people on site forty-nine are private. They've pre-paid for the entire summer and prefer to be self-sufficient. They even take care of their own garbage, so you don't have to worry about that. A trailer came in last week on twenty-three. He seems the quiet sort. He's paid up until the end of July, with the option of staying longer." He repeats what he told me twice before as I nudge him toward the car door.

"Uncle Al, I promise, I remember all of it. I even have it written down, remember?" He'd instructed me to take notes, reminding me in a not so subtle way that, despite my always present good intentions, I have a tendency to get lost in what I'm doing and forget. I give him a kiss on his stubbly cheek and close the door for him. "Drive safe!" I yell after him as he backs out with such speed, he almost knocks over the garbage bin on the other side of the path.

When he disappears into the trees, I turn to the picnic table to grab my camera and swing around to take in my new *domain* through the viewfinder. The caretaker's site is up on a bit of a rise, so you have a good view of the entire campground and the reservoir beyond. On the north side is a small park, with some outdoor grills and picnic tables, right by the boat launch with a small dock for fishing. I'm not able to see a lot of the actual sites, because most of them are at least partially under the cover of trees. But I can see a little of the massive trailer on forty-nine, even though I can see the two tents I know are pitched behind it, along with the silver SUV Uncle Al pointed out. That's the last site and the only one to the right of the dock, with only the woods beyond. Most of the sites have their own water access, especially now with spring run-off making for higher water levels. My uncle keeps track of anyone who comes in with a boat on registration and is adamant about making sure all boats are accounted for at sundown. That's going to be one of my least favorite jobs, since at this time in June; the bugs are legion at dusk. I'm seriously thinking about buying myself one of those mosquito nets and wrapping myself in it. As it is, I'll have to settle for my uncle's fishing cap, which has a little net that drops down to cover my face and neck. I look like a Duck Dynasty widow, but at least I won't get my face chewed off. The rest of my body is a different matter.

The rumble of a motorcycle has me swing my head around. That's got to be number twenty-three. Uncle Al mentioned the Harley Fat Boy, which means as much to me as I'm sure a Michael Kors bag means to him. Not that I like MK bags–I'm more of a

Roots satchel kind of girl myself—but I know *of* them. Without a helmet, the rider's silver gray hair flaps in the wind. Pretty long for an older guy, but you see all sorts here in the mountains. I expect him to ride straight to his site, but instead he turns up this way. Damn, he looks dangerous with the tats running from under the sleeves of his T-shirt, all the way down to his knuckles. Through my camera, I can study each of his features close up. Not quite as old as I initially thought—even though his short beard is as gray as his hair, his face is hardly that of a senior. His eyes are covered with reflective shades, but they do nothing to hide the focus of his stare. I don't even notice I've lowered the camera from my face until he rolls up right in front of me, just inches from my toes.

"Nice Fat Boy," I blurt out nervously, hoping that really is the name of the motorcycle, or else I might have just insulted a sizable biker. He's not a small man, but there's no way he could be mistaken for fat. There's only the slightest hint of some thickening at the waist, and his chest and shoulders are bulky, but with muscle, not fat. The altogether package is fucking intimidating. Over six feet, which is a long way to look up when you've barely cleared five feet yourself, and right now he's standing up to his full height, bulky arms with colorful tattoos firmly folding in front of him. From what I can remember from psych classes in college, this does not make for open and inviting body langue. *Yikes*.

"Your grandfather around?" His voice is not what I expected. Sure, it's raw and rather gruff, but much softer than I would've thought. Almost like someone who is out of breath, yet his breathing seems deep and steady. The question has me bristle up, though. For forever people dismissed me based on my diminutive size and youthful appearance. Drives me nuts.

"Uncle," I correct him sharply, before snapping my mouth shut instantly. *Temper, temper*, I can hear Aunt Kate tut-tutting in my mind. Something she used to say whenever a teenage tantrum took over. Which was only all the time.

I watch as he slowly unfolds his arms and plucks his shades from his strong nose. The clear, ice blue eyes take me by surprise, and my breath hitches at the intensity I see in his scrutiny of my face. "Hmmm," he growls in that strange raspy voice. "Took you for a kid."

I shove my fists in my sides and pull myself up to my full height, such as it is. "Yeah," I say with a forced smile, not quite able to keep the snark out. "I get that a lot. I'm almost forty, FYI. Hardly a kid."

"I'll say." I barely hear his response. I'm too aware of my skin starting to tingle with his leisurely perusal of my attributes. Or lack thereof.

"Anyway, my uncle left. You just missed him." I persist smiling as I vaguely wave at the road, where he disappeared earlier. "Is there anything you need?

I'm taking over for the summer." At that bit of news, the man's full dark eyebrows shoot up.

"You?"

It's a struggle; let me tell you. I'm told I smile all the time, but already this man has me fighting to keep the curve of my mouth up. Better make introductions first, before I decide to use his trailer for target practice.

"Isla Ferris," I say, offering my hand, which he eyes suspiciously like I'm going to infect him with Ebola or something. At this point, I probably would, given the opportunity.

"Ben," he grunts when his eyes finally find their way back to my face. A little hesitant, as if he still doesn't trust my hand is not a weapon of mass destruction, he wraps his big rough mitt around it, swallowing it whole. I'm not sure what it is exactly, that has my stomach doing flip-flops, but we'll blame it on indigestion.

"Site twenty-three, right? Gustafson is you?" I carefully retrieve my hand from his paw as he nods sharply in confirmation. I see conversation with this man will be riveting.

"Running out of firewood," he says with an absolute minimum of words needed to get his message across. My uncle mentioned that he would drive the golf cart down with the occasional load from the pile along the edge of the forest.

"No problem. I'll just load some up and bring it right down." I'm still hanging onto my smile, like the good sport that I am.

"Tomorrow is fine," he says. Without another word, he swings his leg over the bike, kicks back the stand, and starts the thing up. I swear the ground vibrates underneath me as I'm left to stare after his broad back.

Well now. There's a challenge if I ever met one.

CHAPTER 2

I hate surprises.

Despise it when I've just figured out everyone's routines and someone throws a wrench in the wheel. The wrench, in this case, being that little pixie taking the place of Al.

Al was easy: typical ex-military or law enforcement with a need for structure and schedule. He was predictable with his daily routines tightly measured on the clock. Gave me a sense of control that has now been completely obliterated.

Christ, I didn't want to be here in the first place, but got roped back *one last time.* That's what they always say, until the next *next* time. *Fuck*, I'm getting old. Must be, if I'm craving a routine and a comfortable bed myself, instead of living on the fly and trying to sleep on the paper-thin mattress in that ugly old trailer I've called my home for longer than I care to admit.

She was a shocker, all right. I recognized my mistake the moment I took a good look at her. She's tiny. She threw me off with that short-cropped hair, those knee-length, cut-off jeans and tank top, looking more like a teenager. Closer inspection showed the hint of gray in her hairline and the fine wrinkles by her eyes, not to mention the mature fullness of her legs and hips under those loose pants. I'd still not give her a year over thirty, but apparently that's still about ten years off her actual age. I wonder what the heck she's doing here alone, in the middle of nowhere. And what kind of person names their child *Isla*?

This shit has kept me up half the night. The other half I spent traipsing along the waterline through the bush toward the dock. Those fuckers picked a perfect spot to hide out. I want to know what they're up to when they think everyone's asleep.

The sound of wheels on the dirt has me look out the small bedroom window. I knew this chick was going to be an issue. It's not even seven o'clock and here she comes, a blissful smile on her face as she drives her uncle's golf cart right up on my site, a load of wood piling out the back. I stay rooted as she climbs out and starts unloading it beside the firepit, stacking them up neatly. Not that I'm looking at the wood per se, her nicely rounded ass is too distracting for that, but it takes her a while to get them all line up just so, and she's bent over the entire time. A valid explanation—one that makes me feel a bit less like a lecherous old Peeping Tom. Although forty-eight is hardly considered old, it's still a chunk older than *almost forty*, whatever that means.

I must be losing my touch, because I suddenly find myself staring into those hazel eyes I tried not to notice yesterday. She looks a little taken aback when she spots me spying on her. With a final glare, she turns back to the golf cart and I drop the curtain back in front of the window. *Dammit.*

With no hope of getting any sleep now, I pull my jeans on—commando, since I prefer as little constriction as possible these days—and sniff one of the shirts I find on top of the pile on the floor. Good for another day. It's a fucking pain to have to haul stuff down to the laundromat in town. I've tried avoiding it by buying socks and T-shirts in bulk, but with the limited space in this trailer, the garbage bags of dirty laundry piling up seriously cramps my moving room. Not to mention they stink up the place.

I figure she's gone when I prep my percolator with water and grinds and step outside to build a fire. She's not. She's actually stacking what looks to be enough firewood for a bonfire in the firepit. A basket sits on top of the picnic table. *The fuck?*

Maybe I said that out loud, because she whips around with a big toothy grin on her face. "Morning!" she chirps at me, way the hell to cheerfully, this early in the morning. For a minute, I'm frozen on the spot, the coffeepot uselessly clamped in my white-knuckled fist. But when she opens her mouth to speak, I quickly lift my other hand; palm out, to cut her off. I can only take so much talking before my coffee, and she's already blown my limit to hell with '*morning.*'

With a little nod and a wavering smile, she turns back to the firepit and pulls a Zippo out of her back pocket. I've never seen a chick with a Zippo at hand before, and like everything else about her, it throws me off. She builds a good fire, though. The thing lights up like the Fourth of July with one lick of the flame.

The moment she sits down on the other side of the picnic table, I become unstuck and move toward the fire. I flip the grill back on and put my percolator on top, knowing full well it'll take at least ten minutes to produce anything drinkable. Probably be the longest ten minutes of my life.

From the corner of my eye, I watch her open the basket and haul out what looks like...a tray of muffins? Fuck me, I don't eat that stuff for breakfast. I need eggs; preferably with bacon. The smell wafting my way is a good one, though. It promises meat, which is always good in the mornings when I require my protein. Curious now, I turn my full attention to what she's doing and see two plates have appeared with paper napkins and plastic cutlery to the side. She is lifting one of those muffin things out of the tray, except it doesn't look like a muffin, now that I think about it. I slide in across from her, so I can see better, and she slips one of those things on the plate in front of me.

"What is that?" I ask, morning roughness making my voice sound even more hoarse than usual. One of the reasons I don't communicate before I've had a chance to lubricate with hot coffee. I watch her curious eyes flick up from what she's doing.

"Bacon wrapped cheese potato quiches," she says, a little smile playing on her lips.

I know quiche is made with eggs. So basically with bacon, cheese and potato, I've got a one-bite breakfast special. *Good enough for me.* Ignoring the knife and fork, I grab the thing with my hand, noting it is still pretty warm, and pop it in my mouth in one. The pixie's eyes go big as she watches me chomp the whole thing down. *Damn that's good.* I can taste onion and even a hint of jalapeño. Without a word, I grab another from the pan while the girl starts cutting into her own...whatever it is. This time I go slower—just two bites. She's chewing her first bite as I reach over for a third, when suddenly I get my hand slapped.

"Okay," she says, fire in her eyes. "I'm good with the grunting and growling. I'm even good with the hand motions to shut me up; I get caffeine deprivation. But when I come over at the butt crack of dawn to bring over *your* firewood—which I personally loaded and unloaded—and bring you breakfast—which you obviously enjoy, or you wouldn't keep swallowing them down whole; you can at the very least acknowledge it." I look at her for a minute before my eyes are back on the tray of bacon thingies. Before my hand gets halfway there. The tray is yanked away and stuffed back into the basket. "No!" she says firmly. "I already regret doing anything nice for you."

Nice? I guess...I just don't think that much this early. Making coffee is by rote, because that's what I need to get jumpstarted, put food in front of me and I'll down it, no problem—but thinking about the why of things? Most of the time I don't bother; too much fucking work.

"Coffee?" my mouth says, as she walks to the golf cart and puts the basket in the passenger seat. Not sure where that came from, but it seems to work, because she stops halfway in her seat. For a long pause, she seems to contemplate me as I stare back, focusing hard to keep my eyes on her and not let them drift to the basket.

"Milk and sugar?" she says suddenly, putting her hand on the basket's handle. I swear she's holding it hostage, threatening to take it if I can't supply. Which I can...sort of.

"Coffee-Mate," I counter, remembering the old container in the back of one of the tiny kitchen cupboards. It doesn't seem to make her happy, given that she winces like it hurts, but finally she shrugs her shoulders and walks back to the table, with the basket.

Making sure she sits and doesn't move, I hurry inside; grab two mugs, a spoon and the old container of Coffee-Mate that feels like it has a rock at the bottom. I plunk it all on the table, grab the coffee and start pouring. Nice and black, just how I like it. I shove one mug in front of her, while taking a sip of my own. She pulls out the tray and slides another two of those...whatever...on my plate. I watch as she chisels away at the clump of coffee whitener at the bottom of the container, while I eat.

"Next time, I'll bring my own," she grumbles, and my jaw stops moving mid-chew.

Next time?

"You can cook," I point out the obvious. She stares up at me for a second with an eyebrow raised.

"Yes...yes, I can. Your powers of observation are beyond reproach. I guess it's just your communication skills that are sorely lacking." This is all delivered with a smile. I'm starting to enjoy her bite. She may be pint-sized, but she's got the attitude of a linebacker.

"It's good," I say around another bite, and this time her smile is instant and genuine. The difference is stunning. I'm about at my daily quota for interaction, so I eat the rest on my plate silently.

"I'm thinking of making this a daily event," she says, stopping suddenly when she sees what I imagine is panic on my face and promptly bursts out laughing. I stand corrected; her smile is great, her laugh is stunning. With her mouth wide open and her head thrown back, she just lets it rip, not holding a damn thing back. It's rare to see a woman let go like that, maybe with other women, but rarely in the presence of a man. "Freaked you out there for a sec, didn't I?" she teases, still chuckling and shaking her head. "Man, you are so easy." *Easy?* Not something I think I've ever been accused of.

"I mean doing the rounds. A new site every day," she explains. "Kind of like the Welcome Wagon, except instead of useless products and coupons, I bring breakfast."

She lost me there. I have no clue what a Welcome Wagon is, but I do I know I don't like her idea. At all. The thought of her driving up to site forty-nine, with a big smile on her face, has the hair stand up on my neck.

"Not everyone might be as welcoming," I try, but it only serves to make her break out in another bout of laughter. I sit back with my arms crossed over my chest and wait until she's done. It takes a while before she starts wiping at her eyes and calming down.

"Oops, guess you were serious?" she mumbles. "I thought for sure you were joking. I can't imagine anyone being less welcoming than you were. I think most people would love getting an unexpected breakfast served."

Not the folks on forty-nine. I can guarantee that, but I can't say anything.

CHAPTER 3

I haven't seen much of Mr. Congeniality in the past week. Not since I brought him breakfast that morning. The only time I've seen him was when he drove off on his motorcycle and barely raised a hand in greeting when he passed me in the golf cart. Haven't seen him since. Not that I've been listening for the rumble of his bike or anything.

I'd surprised two more sites with breakfast since, but the families at both of those just looked at me strangely. I gave up after realizing my first attempt with Ben was the friendliest reception I've had so far. People are so suspicious, it's depressing. I didn't even try to head over to site forty-nine. Not so much because of my uncle's and Ben's caution to steer clear, but because I'd encountered one of its tenants, while cleaning the showers, one morning. Let's just say it was a less than pleasant experience that left me with the hair on the back of my neck standing on end.

Instead, I've been racking up the shots on my digital card. After I lost my job at the Glenwood Springs Gazette two months ago, I was floundering for a bit before I decided to take it as that proverbial door closing, so I would finally dare to climb out the window. My whole life I've wanted to be a photographer. I took the graduate photography program at ASU, graduated, and subsequently discovered that an education does not a career make. One has to live in the meantime.

So I worked in a photography store for a while, mainly taking pictures of crying babies, until I saw an opening at the paper for a junior staff photographer. It was a pretty steady job, with lots of special event assignments for me, since the one time I was sent out to take pictures of a deadly four-car pile-up on the highway, and I spent my time puking instead of snapping.

My dream has always been realistic art photography; finding beauty in the mundane things around us, capturing the artistry of nature, and showing the brilliance of imperfection. Just so I can open people's narrowed eyes to the richness that surrounds us.

A coffee table book: that's the plan.

It's Plan B, actually, because Plan A—an exhibition of my work at a world-renowned gallery—was too dependent on luck, connections, and patience. All things I do not have in abundance. The book seems like a great alternative. Something that since discovering the new world of self-publishing, has become a distinct possibility. Even if I ever only sell a single copy, the knowledge my vision will be sitting on one coffee table, somewhere in the world, makes my heart full.

My uncle's call for help was the final nudge I needed to get off my keister. I'd caught some beautiful sunsets over the reservoir, and last night, I snapped a bunch of random shots of a little boy, maybe four or so, playing on the dock with a little frog. Against the orange sky it made for a nice contrast. I'll have a closer look at what I've amassed so far this afternoon, but first I want to get some early morning shots with the faint fog rising up off the water as the sun peeks over the mountains.

With one hand reaching for the camera slung around my neck, I stop in my tracks when I hear rustling in the underbrush. It's somewhere to my right, and I slowly turn my body in that direction, while carefully bringing my camera up. About twenty feet away, munching on the young saplings, is the majestic shape of a big, black...cow?

I try to swallow my snicker, but am only partially successful since the beast lifts its massive head and glances my way. Not sure what I was expecting; a bear, or maybe an elk, but the cow is a surprise. Makes for a pretty picture, though, backlit by the early sun, slightly shaking its head to get rid of the bugs buzzing around it. The moment it dives back into its breakfast, I carefully lift the netting of my uncle's fishing cap away from my face and take a peek through the viewfinder, adjusting my shutter speed to the diffused light under the trees. I'd heard them last night, the lowing of the cattle dropped off on the mountain by some local farmer. Livestock grazing on public land is a common practice in Colorado. In fact, when I drove up the mountain last week, I encountered two cowboys on horseback, herding their cattle along the narrow road. Something about a man on horseback...

I lower my camera when I hear a splash in the water beyond, reminding me why I'd come out this early in the first place. The cow forgotten, I make my way to the water's edge to see the light of the sun just starting to streak across the vast expanse of the reservoir. From my vantage point, facing south from the north side of the campground, I can see the dock sticking out from the fog starting to swirl off the water. I take a few shots when I hear another splash. Looking out on the water, I spot a small boat in the middle of the lake, a single person inside. Must be up early to catch some fish, I hear it's the best time of day at dusk or dawn. I wouldn't know, fishing's never been on my list of things I want to do, but I won't scoff at a nice piece of trout or salmon, when offered cleaned and cooked on a plate.

Instead of a fishing rod, the person in the boat seems to be tossing bags overboard. They look like garbage bags. Odd, and a little disturbing. I snap a few pictures but step back into the tree line the moment I see him grab the oars and start rowing back to shore. This way.

Damn. Littering is a big no-no and dumping in the reservoir is seriously frowned upon. Part of me wants to yell out at the boat, but for once, common sense overrules my tendency to speak before thinking. From my perch in the shadow of a sizable tree trunk, I watch him come into shore. Not to the dock, as I expected, but to the only campsite this side of it. Site forty-nine: the site with the elusive tenants.

Curiosity drives me to move closer when the boat disappears from my view. I have yet to set eyes on whoever is living in the trailer and tents. When I sneak up closer, I can hear the low sound of voices and spot two men pulling the boat out of the water on the far side. One is the gentleman, and I use that term loosely, who accosted me in the showers the other day. That's when the smell hits me. The strong stench of ammonia hits my nostrils and almost makes me gag up the quick cup of coffee I had on my way out. *Fucking gross.* I brace myself with a hand on a tree and lift the other to cover my mouth and nose as I watch the two guys make their way to the trailer.

My hand never makes it all to way to my face, when an arm slips around me from behind and a hand, much bigger than mine, firmly covers my mouth.

"Don't move," a gravelly voice whispers right against my ear, sending shivers down my back.

My body is frozen as I'm held in place like that, watching the two men enter the trailer, closing the door behind them. I want to scream for help—and I'm sure I could still make some noise—but something holds me back. Whoever is holding me, starts pulling me back into the woods, and I instinctively start struggling.

"Stop."

Wait a minute.

"You?" My voice is muffled by the hand covering my mouth. My temper rising, I haul back with my elbow and know I hit pay dirt when I hear a satisfying grunt.

"*Jesus*, Pixie."

The arm around my waist is loosened a fraction, and I immediately duck and turn to face the silver-haired biker. *Ben.*

"What the fuck?" I whisper shout. Ben instantly brings his finger to his lips and throws a concerned look over my shoulder. With a sharp shake of his head when I open my mouth, he snags my arm and pulls me further away from the site.

Tromping through the bush, we're almost back to my trailer before he finally lets go of my wrist. Expecting an explanation, I am stunned when he just keeps on walking, leaving me gasping like a fish.

"Hey!" I yell after him, finally finding my voice. When he doesn't stop, I start jogging after him, pulling him around by the arm. "Wait just a damn minute!"

I knew it.

I knew she was trouble the first time I saw her standing there in those ridiculous cut-off jeans. All week I've stayed off her radar, even though I've been keeping an eye out just in case. It wasn't that hard; her damn cheerfulness carries.

My mood wasn't good to start with this morning. Yesterday's covert meeting on the other side of Dolores didn't quite go as I had hoped. My hopes to move full steam ahead, and get this last one over with, were thwarted when I was told to hold off taking them down. Goddamn desk-jockeys always want to hold out for the big fish. According to an informant, said big fish was expected to make an appearance sometime soon. In the meantime I'm stuck with the two guys I've been keeping my eye on. Keeping a low profile for the benefit of whoever is looking, and at the same time, keeping a sharp eye out for anyone getting too close to the compound.

This is what I'm good at, blending in with the biggest lowlifes on the face of the earth. Doesn't matter that getting close to that kind of scum makes me feel as filthy as the pond they crawled from.

Last time. With early retirement waiting for me on the other side, I take in a deep breath and consider how to keep this nosy little chick out of the line of fire. Another sacrifice for the sake of the greater good. Except the plan that comes to mind doesn't feel anywhere near what a sacrifice is supposed to feel like. I should know—I've made many.

"What the hell was that all about?" she snaps, her little fists bunched on her healthy hips, and her camera dangling between what looked to be two scant handfuls. Just enough.

"Two men alone on the remotest site of the campground, who work hard at staying out of the way, and you think it's a good idea to go spying on them?" I counter, stringing more words together than I have since I hit my twenties. My voice strains with them, and I lift a hand to the scar at my throat, partially hidden by the beard and the extensive tattoos reaching my jawline. The little pixie's eyes follow my movements, and I have a feeling she's more observant than I'm comfortable with.

"I was just shooting the sunrise," she says defensively. "Got curious when I saw one of them on the lake this early." She takes a step closer and tilts her head to one side, the ridiculous hat in danger of slipping off. "Did you know they're dumping shit in the reservoir? Who does that? Why would someone throw their trash out of a boat, when there are perfectly good dumpsters at the end of the road? I know Uncle Al said they take care of their own garbage, but I'm pretty sure he has no idea they're tossing it in the reservoir." She prattles on in a suspicious voice. Proving that she is smarter than is good for her. Son of a bitch.

"Just stay clear of them. I'll keep an eye out," I enforce, giving her a stern look, which is received with a roll of her expressive hazel eyes behind the mosquito netting. No damn respect.

"You know, you make it really hard to maintain my positive attitude. I'm in need of more coffee—you're killing my buzz." With that, she whips around on her bright orange, Converse high tops, grabbing at the fishing hat that almost comes sailing off her head. With attitude too big for that short little body, she stalks off, and I can't help staring after the enticing sway of her generous hips in those ridiculous jeans.

CHAPTER 4

So much for killing with kindness.

The man aggravates me way too much to muster up any kind of kindness.

Bossy, controlling, and grumpy! Other than, "*You can cook*," last week, when I brought him breakfast—and that wasn't even all that convincing—all he's done is either criticize me or ignore me. I'm done trying.

All day I've been holed up in the trailer with my laptop, editing some of my photos from this past week in Lightroom. At this rate I'll have a coffee table book a week. I'm really pleased with the way most of these have turned out. It's not until I come across a covert picture I took of Ben, driving past me on his bike one day, that my irritation with him bubbles up again. How dare he look so...super hot? A silver fox on a bike—and yet all the attraction disappears after discovering his serious lack of personality. Okay, well maybe not *all*.

Ugh. I slam my laptop shut and go hunt for something to eat. The sun is already setting low in the sky, and I have plans to experiment a little tonight with night skies. Something I've not been very successful with thus far, but I'm hoping with my tripod and new wide aperture lens, I'll have more luck. The tripod is necessary, because free-handing the low shutter speeds you need to capture the light is impossible, I discovered. The lens should help with depth perception.

I'm sorely disappointed when I pull open the fridge door. All I have left is a few eggs, two slices of ham, and a loaf of bread in the little freezer. Resigned, I throw together a few sandwiches with fried eggs, the ham, and some mayo. Along with a couple of bottles of water, I stuff them in my backpack. The bug spray goes in a side pocket, and I strap a rolled up sleeping bag under the flap. All my camera equipment is already in there. It's still warm out, but I still dress for the cooler air later, and the bugs waiting to eat me alive. Old sweats, tucked into my high tops, a thin rain slicker over my long-sleeved T-shirt, and my uncle's fishing hat finishes the ensemble. I couldn't care less, as long as I keep those bloodthirsty mosquitoes from poking more holes in me. The jacket hits me halfway down my legs, which is good because the backs of my thighs are already full of bumps and lumps. Little bastards.

I forfeit the golf cart, and instead, hoof my way down to the dock, toting the backpack over my shoulder. I wave at the few families gathered around their respective firepits, but most have gone inside now that the bugs are out. There's hardly any wind, which doesn't help.

No one is on the dock, and other than a lone kayaker passing by on the water, I don't see another soul out here. I cast a furtive glance in the direction of the trailer on site forty-nine, or at least what I can see of it, but there are no lights on inside, nor is there a fire burning.

The sun is starting to slip behind the mountains, turning the sky a fiery red, and I quickly retrieve the camera from my pack. As soon as it disappears entirely, I can feel the cooler air settling in. I quickly assemble my tripod and switch out the lens on the camera, while I still have some natural light. Of course, I didn't think to bring a flashlight. *Rookie.* I make the legs on the tripod as short as I can, thinking it'll be easier to lie on my stomach when I take the shots. Once that's done, I spread out my sleeping bag and pull out a sandwich and bottle of water.

The night is quiet, only interrupted by the occasional call of the frogs, and rare lowing of cattle on the mountain. My egg sandwich is still lukewarm, and hits the spot as I enjoy the quiet lapping of the water under the dock.

"What's for dinner?"

I scramble to my feet, almost toppling off the edge of the dock in the water, if not for Ben's large hand grabbing me by my upper arm.

"*Jesus!*" I power hiss. "You keep scaring the snot out of me." I want to turn my back but am too distracted by the twinkle in those ice blue eyes of his. That and the fine lines fanning out from them almost make him look mellow. Determined, I tear my gaze away from him and sit down on my sleeping bag, facing the water. Upset at the disruption of my peaceful evening, I chomp down on my sandwich.

"Got any more of those?" I hear his raspy voice behind me, along with the rustling of my backpack. I whip my head around, just as he pulls out my second sandwich.

"Hey, that's mine!"

"I'll bring you dessert later." He shoves half the sandwich down his gullet. "Haven't had dinner yet, I'm starving," he mumbles with his mouth full.

I try to shut him out, but find myself handing him the second water bottle instead. My temper flares like fireworks but dies down just as fast. I just don't have it in me to stay mad. I have to say, this is the first time I actually appreciate his general lack of communication. I almost forget he's there as I make myself comfortable, stuffing my backpack under my arms for support as I start tweaking the settings on my camera. I barely notice him lying down beside me, only looking over once to find him staring up at the sky, his hands folded behind his head.

It's not quite dark enough but still I start snapping away when the first stars become visible.

Without the light pollution you have in most towns and cities, the skies out here are amazingly clear. I have hooked up a remote trigger to the camera to avoid any movement at all and start snapping.

"Did you see that?" I whisper, after I watched a falling star cut across the sky.

"Hmmm," Ben growls. I slightly turn my head to look at him. He's on his side on an elbow; his head supported by his hand and his focus is on me, not the sky.

"I can't believe you missed it," I huff, a little unnerved by his scrutiny.

"Didn't miss a thing."

Damn, she's irresistible.

Even in that outrageous outfit she's wearing, flapping her hand at the bugs buzzing around her, she radiates personality. It won't exactly be a hardship to keep her close.

The big eyes she makes at me through the netting in front of her face almost makes me chuckle. Almost, but not quite. Just over her shoulder, I notice some movement on the edge of the water; right in front of the mini-compound I've been keeping an eye on. Just a shadow, but I see him.

I know there's a third man slipping in and out over the water in the rowboat, presumably to avoid anyone noticing. I noticed. It's my job to notice. As much as I'd managed to insert myself with Luis and Carlos, the two guys running a lucrative business from the campground, they'd never even hinted at the third guy. To them I'm just the hired muscle, recommended by a mutual acquaintance to keep an eye out while they work. Of course, they don't know I keep an eye on them at the same time.

In fact, this morning, when I ran into Isla, I'd been checking out their early morning activities. The boat had been pulled into the brush on the shoreline, but there was no sign of the third man. I watched as the two men loaded up the garbage bags and saw Carlos rowing out to the middle of the lake, dumping the garbage bags overboard. It had the hair on the back of my neck stand on end. That's when I spotted Isla doing a poor job of hiding in the tree line, and sneaking up on the site, as the boat came into shore.

I'd been pissed.

Her curiosity is dangerous. I wouldn't put it past her to march in on a situation that could end disastrously for her. But it leaves me in a rough spot. Al would've been easy to deal with, being ex-law enforcement. I'd planned on giving him a head's up before making a move. His nosy, but cute as fuck, niece is a different thing.

I'm going to need to keep the men's attention away from Isla, and her focus off them. So that means keeping her otherwise occupied. The last won't be a hardship, but the first might prove difficult. Luis has more than once made some crude remarks, which made it clear he is very aware of the pretty camp manager.

"You're easy to look at, Pixie," I quickly say, when she starts turning in the direction of the silent shadow at the water's edge. Instead, her head whips back in my direction and if possible, those eyes are spread even wider.

"You're giving me whiplash, you know?" she says finally. "Have you ever been diagnosed with multiple personality disorder? Because I think I've met a few of them already." This time I can't hold back, despite the still figure in my peripheral vision, I let out a gruff chuckle. "And what's with calling me Pixie?" she continues undeterred. "Must you remind me constantly how short, boyish, and unfeminine I am? Trust me, I already know. No need to rub it in."

"You're nuts," I conclude, when she hits me over the head with that one. "I don't see that when I call you Pixie. You're very sexy, a bit otherworldly, full of energy, cheerful—kind of plucky." Not sure where that all came from, but it sounds good.

"Oh," she says a bit dumbfounded, but quickly recovers. "Plucky? How does a badass like you carry around a word like *plucky* in their vocabulary?"

When she starts pushing up from the sleeping bag, drawing unwanted attention to herself; I do the only thing I can think of. I pull her down on top of me, pull that weird hat off her face, and kiss her.

The moment she lands on top of me, she stiffens up like a board, but when my mouth touches hers, I feel her body relax and mold to mine. I should be keeping an eye on our quiet observer, but the slow glide of lips on lips is distracting. Very distracting. As is the little hitch in her breathing when I open my mouth slightly and draw in her plump bottom lip. Her small hands start off pressed palm down against my chest, but are now fisting in my shirt, hanging on.

Suddenly she pulls back, and I make no effort to hold on, letting her lift her head. Her face only inches from mine, she stares in my eyes. Looking for something—what, I don't know. Whatever it is, I'm guessing she finds it, because the next second; she's kissing me with a heat her temper only hinted at, openmouthed and with a passion that knocks me off my feet. Without thinking, I press her against me, one hand on her ass, the other cupping the back of her head, and my tongue slipping inside her hot mouth.

Christ.

I'm fucked six ways to Sunday.

The little pixie is on fire, and I can't help the deep groan that bubbles up from my gut. She feels small under my hands, her head almost swallowed up by the spread of my fingers against her scalp. Her lips slick and pliable, while her sharp little tongue twists around mine. Squirming against me, her body is like a furnace in the cool night. I almost miss the slight shift in the air. Almost, but not quite. Pulling my lips from her, I use my hand to tuck her head in my neck, while my eyes quickly scan the trees on the edge of the water to our north.

Gone. The shadow I'm sure was Luis has disappeared. Seeing me make out with the object of his desire surely won't go over too well, but I'll take whatever comes my way as long as it keeps his attention off her.

I lay my head back, trying hard to catch my breath, just like the small woman sprawled on top of me. I'm perfectly content to simply lie there, the heat of her soaking into my skin. When she starts moving, pressing against my hold, I let my arms fall away and watch as she slides off me. There's no way I can hide my body's response to that hot as fuck kiss, so I'm not surprised to hear the startled shock in her breathing when she brushes her leg against my painfully hard cock.

I silently fold my arms behind my head again and observe Isla trying to straighten herself out, avoiding looking at me. That's okay. I'm not quite sure what to say after that myself.

I watch as she dissembles her camera with shaking hands, shoving the pieces in her pack, along with the ridiculous hat. I get to my feet when she does, and wait while she expertly rolls the sleeping bag, securing it under the flap of her backpack.

Slinging it over her shoulder, she starts walking away without having said a single word. That's not okay. I quickly fall in step and lift the pack off her shoulder and onto mine. That earns me a furtive glance before she focuses back on the path in front of her. The only sound is the crunch of our footsteps on the gravel as we make our way to her trailer.

Once there, she climbs the two steps, opens the door and turns with her hand held out. "Thanks for carrying that," she says, but her eyes are somewhere in the middle of my chest.

"Go inside," I order her, not about to have her withdraw from me now. With a gentle push, I force her to back up inside. I follow her into the trailer, closing the screen behind me. Dumping her bag on the seat, I quickly take in my surroundings. A small kitchen with a banquette and table on my right, a couch in front of me, to my left the door to a bathroom I guess, and a bedroom beyond. Much more luxurious quarters than my ratty trailer. When my eyes come back to Isla, she's peeking at me from under her eyelashes, her teeth worrying her still swollen lips.

"Don't." I reach out and stroke the pad of my thumb over the ridges her teeth left behind.

"What was that?" she finally speaks, her voice softer than I've heard it before.

"A start," I tell her, leaning in to brush my lips against hers in a quick taste. "That was a start."

I leave her standing there, her gorgeous mouth hanging open, as I close the door behind me and walk away from temptation.

CHAPTER 5

"Two pounds of ground beef, please."

Weekday mornings at the Dolores Food Market are blissfully quiet. That tends to change on the weekend when visitors flood the small town. And a small town it is, its inhabitants quick to embrace any summer 'locals,' as judged by the friendly waves, nods, and hellos I've encountered this morning. Only my third time in the store and already I'm welcomed like a regular. I love that sense of community.

The beef is for the meatloaf I'm planning to make for dinner, along with the baking potatoes, and makings for a salad I'm toting in my basket. I tell myself I'm cooking for a few days at a time, when I order more meat than I usually consume in a week. It's got nothing to do with a certain confounding man, whose imprint I can still feel on my lips after days. Nothing at all.

"Thank you." I smile at the woman behind the counter when she hands me my package. Tossing it in my basket, I head to the dairy cooler to pick up some eggs and cream cheese to go with the apples I already picked up. I have maple syrup at the trailer, along with a bag of almonds and some desiccated coconut; the makings of a new cheesecake recipe I want to try out. For myself.

Cursing myself for not grabbing a cart instead, I tote the overfull basket to the check out.

I had to get away from the campground this morning. Normally, I clean the few showers and outhouses this time of the morning, but after another restless night, I needed a change of scenery. I stuff the bags in the backseat of my Beetle and climb behind the wheel, just as a familiar rumble hits my ears. Halfway in the car, I turn my head and watch as Ben pulls his bike up right behind my ride. No escape.

My uncle taught me the best defense is a good offense.

"Did you follow me?" I snap. Okay, so not a great offense, given the smirk on his face.

"Purely coincidental," he claims, lifting three fingers in what I know to be scout's honor. The rugged-looking biker dude in front of me is so far from a Boy Scout; I burst out laughing. "Ahhh," he says, a full smile that has my breath catch in my throat, on his face. "There she is. Was wondering where she'd gone."

Good Lord.

The man left me breathless a couple of nights ago with promises of more to come—unless I grossly mistook his meaning—and promptly ignored me. Until now.

A quiet broody Ben is a challenge, but an actual communicating Ben has me mentally toss the towel in the ring. Why even try to resist? Especially when his delicious mouth forms such nice words. I'm a weakling, and I know it. That mouth on mine, those strong white teeth nibbling at my lips, that silky tongue stroking mine into submission; I'm a puddle. I knew it before, I know it now—resistance is futile. It's been too damn long.

With a deep sigh, I give in. "I'm making meatloaf and cheesecake tonight. Aiming to have it on the table at seven." Not waiting for an answer, I finish getting in the car, but I get one anyway.

"Not gonna say no—I've tasted your cooking," he calls after me, right before I slam the door shut. In my rearview mirror I see him back away from my bumper and with a roar, take off down the road.

I need liquor—lots and lots of liquor. With that in mind, I turn my car in the opposite direction where I know GST Liquor will have just what the doctor ordered.

By the time I get back up the mountain, it's lunchtime. I'd made a quick stop at The Pony Express in town, a great little bakery/coffee shop for some coffee and a bagel to go. I noticed some great photography on the walls and got to talking with the owner. She actually asked to see some of my work, and I'm pretty pumped to get some shots printed to show her.

After storing my groceries, I sit down at the picnic table outside the trailer, with my coffee and the bagel I've been drooling over since they prepared it for me. Slathered with a thick layer of cream cheese, sautéed leeks, and thinly sliced smoked salmon, it tastes like heaven.

Two more groups of campers show up this afternoon, one a bunch of rambunctious young guys I'll likely have to keep an eye and an ear on. They look like they're poised for a rowdy stay. The second sign in is a nice, outdoorsy couple, if the bikes and kayaks attached to their SUV are any indication. I make sure I assign them a site that is nowhere near the group of potential troublemakers.

With the bathrooms and showers cleaned, and the cheesecake in the oven, I have some time to go over the images I'd like to get printed up. I'll likely have to head into Cortez for that. Scrolling through my shots on the laptop, I happen upon the couple of pictures I took of the rowboat the other morning. Looking carefully, I notice something I didn't notice at the time; the bags look heavy from the way whoever was in the boat is handling them. What on earth are they dumping? I print off a copy on regular paper on my small printer, wondering if I should give my uncle a call on how to proceed. If they are dumping in the lake and whatever is in those bags is harmful to the environment; that could be a big problem. This reservoir is used for irrigation water not only for Dolores County, but Montezuma County as well.

I've just printed off copies of all the shots I have when the timer on the oven goes off. It smells amazing when I open the oven. At first glance, it looks like a regular New York cheesecake, but it hides an Amaretto apple compote I made in the middle. The crust of ground almond and coconut, lined with a very thin layer of white chocolate, will hopefully give it a little crunch.

With dessert ready, I head outside to start a nice hot fire in the pit. Once I have it going hot, I toss the potatoes wrapped in a double layer of tinfoil straight into the hot embers. Once that's done, it takes me just ten minutes to throw together the meatloaf in a covered cast iron pan and slide it on top of the grill.

I just step inside to get started on the salad when I hear Ben's bike rumbling by and a hint of nerves starts swirling in my stomach.

Whatever she's cooking it smells fucking phenomenal from way the hell over here.

After running into town on an errand for Luis, picking up supplies, I'm in desperate need of a shower to wash off the stench from the unsavory characters I've had to interact with.

He'd been pissed the morning after he spotted Isla and me on the dock. It took everything out of me not to reach out and snap his wrist when he stuck a gun in my face. Instead, I'd simply stood my ground quietly and waited until he finally lowered the gun, hopefully deciding she wasn't worth the trouble. He'd been ignoring me since, so I was surprised when he texted me first thing this morning with a grocery list.

I'd already surmised they had to be exchanging supplies with product by way of that damn rowboat. The fact they sent me off to pick up rock salt and bleach solidified my concern about what happened to the third guy. I'd managed to get message out that we might be dealing with a dead body at the bottom of the reservoir earlier this week, but it wasn't something that could be dealt with right away, without blowing my cover.

I stop the bike on the path beside Isla's site and leave it running, while I pull a bottle of wine out of the saddlebags, set it on her picnic table, and get back on.

"Back soon," I mouth at her over the noise of my engine, while she stands in the doorway watching my every movement with curiosity, salad tongs in her hand.

It takes me five minutes to shower and pull on a clean set of clothes, and I'm back outside, this time leaving the bike behind.

I can hear her swearing up a storm from a distance and pick up the pace. The bottle I left on the table has been uncorked and has two glasses upside down beside it. A salad bowl with one of those net thingies, to keep out the bugs, is sitting on the table, as are plates and eating tools. It's nice. It's also been a fuck of a long time since I've sat down to a proper home-cooked meal. The unfamiliar warmth in my gut sours when I consider who might be watching.

"Dammit!" I hear her mutter as she sticks her entire arm in the firepit.

"The fuck are you doing?"

She jumps back at my voice and immediately squeals as her arm hits the side of the metal pit. *For fuck's sake.* I'm beside her in two steps and haul her with me into her trailer, straight to the kitchen where I stick her arm under the tap.

"That was your fault!" she snaps. "You creep up every time, scaring the living daylights out of me," she hisses and pulls her arm from under the water.

"Keep it there," I instruct her, rummaging through the little freezer to look for a bag of peas, or ice, or something, but all I find is half a loaf of bread and a Ziploc bag full of double A batteries. I hold it up and raise my eyebrow in question. "Emergency stash?" Isla rolls her eyes in response.

"Power goes off regularly," she explains. "Uncle Al has a generator in the shed outside, but he likes to be prepared. Nothing quite as exciting as where your mind went."

I pull out a frost-covered, forgotten, ice cube tray and have to whack it against the counter a few times to get them to dump in the towel. "That's too bad," I whisper against the shell of her ear, as I step up behind her and turn off the water, pressing the makeshift ice pack against the red welt on her forearm. I can feel her bristle, but she doesn't say a thing. A quiet grin slips on my face.

After fishing the potatoes from the fire—the task Isla had been trying to accomplish—I sit down across from her at the table. She's already poured some wine, and although not my drink of choice, I don't mind a glass when the occasion calls for it. A generous chunk of meatloaf, making my mouth water, is barely deposited on my place when I shovel a bite in my mouth. *Fucking amazing.*

She puts me on the spot when she asks what I do for a living, but seems satisfied when I tell her I'm a semi-retired government employee. Not exactly the truth, but not quite a lie either. Apparently she notices my reluctance to talk, because she starts telling me about her photography. Something she's obviously passionate about.

Dinner is comfortable. Any tension from earlier appears to be gone, and I sit back, listening to Isla talk about her visit to that funky bakery in town. It feels good, chilling, sharing a meal—all the more so because it's with her. She's unlike anyone I've ever known. A take life by the balls kind of attitude you don't see very often. Even so, I sense there is something underneath that almost exaggerated zest for life she shows. Something sad.

"Good grief, I've been yapping your ear off. Do you want some coffee with dessert?"

"Depends on what's on the menu." I mentally slap myself for letting that slip out. Even in the dimming light, I can see a blush staining Isla's cheeks. "Coffee'd be good," I add quickly. "And you're ten out of ten on what you've fed me so far, so dessert would be a yes."

She shakes her head slightly, trying to hide her small smile at the compliment. "You're weird," she states boldly. "Most of the time, you grunt or give monosyllabic answers, and then out of the blue you give me entire compound sentences." She's teasing—mostly.

"I don't talk much," I confirm, my fingers lightly tracing the scar under my beard and once again her eyes follow my movements. "Don't like to waste energy on empty words. But I like to listen to you talk." She lets out a nervous chuckle before getting up from the table.

"I'll be right back."

While she's inside, I take the opportunity to scan the site I've been trying to keep my eye on. Lights appear to be on in the trailer, and I don't see any movement, although that's no guarantee. For all I know they've had eyes on us the entire time.

"Ben?"

I turn around to find Isla hanging out the trailer door.

"Is it okay if we have coffee inside? It's getting a bit buggy out there."

"No problem." I get up, grab our now empty glasses and plates and follow her inside.

I can tell by her jerky movements she's nervous having me in her space, which is unfortunate, since I've developed a liking to being in her *space.*

"Sit." She waves impatiently at the banquette in the small kitchen. Instead, I take a seat on the couch. With purpose. The moment she turns, two mugs in her hands, I can see panic flit over her face. Just as quickly as it appeared, it's gone. Replaced with a dramatic eye roll. I chuckle and hold out my hand for the coffee, taking a sip, and setting it down on the narrow coffee table. She's back in seconds with a massive piece of cheesecake.

"That's a fuck of a lot of cheesecake, Pixie," I point out, looking at what appears to be a quarter cake.

"Sweet things have to be devoured—not nibbled at," she says sagely, sitting down as far from me as she can manage and immediately digs in.

"Not gonna argue that," I agree, my eyes firmly focused on her and not my plate. When she finally feels me watching, she looks at me from under her lashes and immediately turns pink. "But first let me enjoy this." I pile a huge bite on my fork, and stuff it in my mouth. *Christ*. This is good. Watching her eat, hearing her little moans of pleasure, is enough to have me inhale mine. I'm glad somewhere there's another half to this cake, because I'm too preoccupied with those whimpers of ecstasy to taste much.

"Done?" I lean over and pluck the empty plate from her hands, setting it next to mine on the table. She promptly reaches out for her coffee, but I catch her hand mid-air. "Later," I whisper as I bridge the vast space she's put between us and pull her right up on my lap. "Much later," I say, holding on to her tight, because she's squirming to get off.

"Ben! I'm heavy," she squeals.

I throw my head back and laugh. "Babe, you weigh nothing."

"Hardly. I've got a big ass; I'm a size fourteen." Like that's supposed to mean anything to me.

"So? You've got a big ass. I like that about you," I tell her honestly, pulling one leg over my lap so she's straddling me, and cupping said ass with both my hands. She's got a great ass. Lots to grab onto.

I can tell she's contemplating getting mad, I can see it on her face, but then a smile breaks through as she leans into me. "That's good," she whispers, just a breath away from my mouth, before closing the gap and kissing me. To show her just how much I like it,

I slip my hands in the back of her waistband, squeezing her firm flesh. I swallow her gasp when I twist both of us and end up with my hips between her legs. One hand still tucked in the back of her pants and the other pulling her leg over my hips, I grind my length against her center. The slight tug of her fingers tangling in my hair, and the other hand clutching my ass, she encourages me to move. *Fuck me.* With her tongue in my mouth, her nails scratching my ass cheek, where she's worked her hand down the back of my jeans, and her heat rubbing against my dick, I'm about to explode.

"God, baby—you feel fucking fantastic..." I mumble in her mouth when I suddenly feel her go rigid beneath me. I reluctantly lift my mouth from hers and watch her turn her head slightly—listening. Then I hear it, too.

A car revving its engine.

CHAPTER 6

God, I'm frustrated.

Last time I checked my clock, it was one-thirty in the morning. Not even a round with my little battery-operated friend—the one I claimed earlier not to have—did the trick. It got me off so fast, after having Ben work me up like that; it barely brought any relief. *Bastard.*

The moment he heard the car engine, he was up and out the door, only stopping to give me stern instructions not to move. I wasn't about to listen, though. In a flash, I was out the door behind him. At the sound of the screen door slamming shut, he'd stopped and turned before stalking back, not stopping until he was right up in my space.

I heard it then, the ruckus coming from the direction of where those damn kids pitched their tents.

"I've got it," I told Ben, trying to step by him. After all, this was part of the job. But his hand snuck out and grabbed my wrist, swinging me back around.

"Wrong," he said, pissing me way the hell off, as I tilted my head back to look into his angry eyes. "I'll deal with them. You go in and go to bed."

To say that was a slap in the face is mild. Rejection fucking sucks, and his face was completely closed down. Cold. Not even a hint of the fire I saw there just minutes ago. Well, fuck him. He let me go easily that time when I yanked my hand back. Fighting down the telltale burn in my eyes, I lifted my chin and squared my shoulders. He wanted to deal with a bunch of drunken idiots? *Fine, let him.*

Without a word, I swung around and marched back to the trailer, slammed the door shut, and had a good cry over the sink, cleaning the dishes. The hot and cold routine he was giving me was not something I needed in my life. My head was done...my body, not so much.

Since then things have been quiet; not a peep from the guys on site twelve, but also no sign of Ben. I'm so stupid. Guess part of me was waiting for him to come back, but he never did. Color me a fool. Again.

Sleep won't come and I've tried reading, tried watching some TV on the little thirty-year-old set, complete with rabbit ears, but the single working channel was so snowy, I couldn't tell whether I was watching CNN or the Playboy Channel. So now it's back to rolling around in the surprisingly comfortable queen-sized bed.

The sound of something moving over the gravel path leading to my campsite has me sitting straight up in bed. Is Ben coming back after all? With my ears perked, I hold my breath, waiting for the sound of the storm door. It feels like I'm waiting minutes when in fact only a few seconds have probably passed. *There*. A distinct crash sounds right outside the window at the foot of my bed. Gingerly, without making too much noise myself, I crawl over the bed to take a peek. I carefully pull the curtain aside and press my nose against the small pane of glass. The moon is not out tonight, so it's pretty dark out, just the faint light from the shower building, a couple of hundred yards away, on the other side of the trailer. I don't see anything, only the familiar shape of the picnic table and a glint off the metal from the firepit next to it. *Dammit!* My cast iron pan is still sitting on top of the grill. Rookie mistake.

I quickly jump out of bed, pull on a pair of sweats, stick my feet in boots I find on the floor, and shuffle to the door with a flashlight in my hands. Pushing open the door, I shine my light over the picnic table and the pit beyond. Nothing. Better get that pan inside or whatever's out there will be keeping me up all night. Letting the storm door fall shut behind me, I hurry to the firepit, where the lid is half shoved off my cast iron pan. I straighten out the lid, and with my flashlight in one hand and the pan in the other, I turn to hurry back inside but freeze in my tracks instead.

I never heard it, and I certainly didn't see it when I stepped out, but there's no missing it now. Standing on the edge of the path is a sizable black bear. I should've brought the shotgun Uncle Al keeps beside the bed. The shotgun I promised to practice with but didn't.

"Hey!" I hear yelled, followed by a sharp whistle. Next thing I know, a gunshot cracks through the night and instinctively I drop everything I have in my hands and drop to the ground, balling myself up as small as I can. A loud grunt and more yelling, but I'm not listening. Instead I find myself eye to eye with a small bear cub, sitting under the picnic table, the little culprit.

I'm in trouble.

"Pixie! Get the fuck inside. Slowly." I can hear Ben's voice from the other side of the momma bear, who is swaying from side to side, her head turning back and forth between the cub and me on one side, and Ben, who is waving his arms in the air on the other. "I've got you, baby, just go easy."

Carefully I crawl sideways on hands and knees, my eyes now focused on the mother. I stop every time she looks my way, like a game of Marco Polo. Except the stakes are a little higher. With each shift of my body, I move a little closer to the steps, and a little further from blocking momma bear from her cub. I'm so focused on her, and on the stairs, I don't notice the cub until the thing toddles into my view and hobbles past me to its mother's side. Immediately momma bear takes off behind the trailer, her little one hurrying to keep up.

"Isla," I hear Ben's voice. "Go inside, babe. I'll be right there, just gonna make sure they don't turn back." The moment he too disappears behind the trailer, I scramble up the steps and launch myself through the door, slamming it shut behind me.

It takes longer than I expect. The bears take their time disappearing into the woods at the far side of the campground. On the way back, I have to contend with worried campers who woke up when I fired a warning shot in the air. I made sure every last one of them was instructed on the rules of camping in bear country. Something I didn't do myself when I took the plates in but forgot about the pan. *Christ*, if I hadn't been able to distract her, I would've had to shoot that magnificent animal. As it is, I attracted too much attention already, judging by the lights on in the trailer on the far side of the campground. No doubt they've taken note of the fact I'm carrying.

In contrast, Isla's trailer is dark, which is a bit of a surprise. I would've thought she'd have the place lit up like a football stadium. An unfamiliar pang of guilt hits me when I think of the way I walked out on her earlier. *Fuck me*, but I want her.

Realizing I hadn't even heard the loud raucous party, I managed to break up in record time, had freaked me the fuck out. I never lose sight of my surroundings, ever. But I had then; so wrapped up in the pint-sized sweetness moaning under me I wouldn't have heard a bomb go off. It threw me; I walked away, and regretted it almost instantly. Even more so, when I fucking spent hours sitting in my trailer after, staring up the hill through the tiny window.

My life has never been conducive to having anything more than the occasional one-night stand. The only time I spent more than one night with someone, since I started working undercover, was when it benefited the case I was working on at the time. Just like I'd planned to do with Isla. I had no trouble keeping my mind focused where it should be on those previous occasions. Not so now. Not even after I left her alone.

The campground is quiet now. The occasional frog the only sound to be heard. The storm door squeaks when I pull it open. The same sound I'd heard from my trailer earlier, causing me to run up here, to find Isla in a damn standoff between the bear and her cub. I knock softly on the door so I don't scare her, before trying the knob, finding it unlocked. It's dark, so I let my eyes adjust for a second before checking the kitchen and the couch. Then I turn left, toward the bedroom. Only to find it empty as well.

"Isla?"

I hear it then, a slight shuffle, right before the narrow bathroom door flings open. I barely manage to catch her when she comes barreling out of her hiding place and launches herself against me, shaking like a leaf.

"*Fuck, fuck, fuck...*" I hear her mumbled voice in my neck. She's on me like Velcro, her legs wrapped around my hips and her arms so tight around my neck; she's cutting off airflow. With her body attached to mine, I make my way into the bedroom. One hand on her ass and one planted in the bed, I climb in with her hanging off me like a monkey, boots and all.

"Shhh..." I roll on my back and take her with me. "Easy, girl." My hand firmly rubs the length of her spine, with long even strokes.

For the longest time I do just that, until finally her shakes slow down to an occasional shiver, and her rapid breath becomes more regular.

"I'm an idiot."

Not quite sure that was the first thing I expected to hear from her mouth, it catches me off guard. I can't help but chuckle. "How's that?" I ask, my voice worse than normal as a result of the earlier yelling and talking I've done.

"Left the pan outside. I should know better. Fuck, I *do* know better. I can't believe I did that," she rambles without lifting her head.

"Nah," I brush her off. "I was the last one in. Should've grabbed it, but I was in too much of a hurry to follow you inside."

"Yeah," she says, pushing herself off me and piercing me with her eyes. "Ironic, isn't it? Cause half an hour later, you were in an even bigger hurry on your way out. Which makes me an even bigger idiot." The last she mutters under her voice, but I catch it. It doesn't make me feel good. I normally don't care enough to worry about people's feelings getting bruised, but I sure as hell don't like being responsible for the hurt I put on her. Damn, has she been crying?

"I made a mistake," I admit, but am confused when she scrambles from the bed, walking straight to the door and swinging it open.

"I got that the first time you took off," she says, her eyes on me angry, but not enough to mask the pain swimming in her unshed tears. "So I'll make it easy on you. Get. The fuck. Out." Every word is punctuated with a hitch in her breath, and I can see the hard fight to keep her composure playing out on her face.

Keeping my eyes on hers, I swing my legs over the side, get up, and walk toward the door, which she resolutely holds open for me. The little squeal, when I pull the door from her hand and firmly close it, is the only sound from her before I have her up in my arms and carry her straight back to bed.

I use the bulk of my body to keep hers from going anywhere. "Let me explain something, since it would appear the message didn't get through. The mistake wasn't kissing you, I made a mistake when I walked away."

Her mouth opens in a silent *ohh*, and I use the opportunity to kiss her deeply. I've always been more of a *show* than a *tell* kind of guy.

I know the moment her hands curve around my back and slide up under my shirt, that whatever happens, there's no way I'll be able to walk away from her this time. Breathing hard already, I force myself up on my knees and yank my shirt over my head. Isla runs her tongue along her freshly kissed bottom lip and reaches out to run her fingers through the hair on my chest.

"You're silver everywhere," she mutters.

"Not everywhere," I growl, pulling the gun from my waistband and tossing it on the nightstand. My hands work impatiently at the buttons of my jeans, and I quickly stand up to divest myself of the rest of my clothes.

"Commando," she sighs, as her eyes slide down to where my cock stands out hard from the only hair on my body that's still the original color. The rest of me turned gray when I hit thirty-five, almost overnight.

"Only way to go," I rumble, climbing back on the bed and over her. "Now let's see about you."

My need to get her naked has me pulling those ugly as sin sweatpants down her legs, tossing them on top of the growing pile of clothes on the floor. When I tuck my fingers in the sides of her panties, she's already got her shirt up over her head, and by the time that's gone, she's as naked as the day she was born. I sit back on my haunches between her legs, placing my hand on her chest, just below her neck. Her heartbeat hammers against the palm of my hand, and I can almost reach the width of her shoulder with the span of my fingers. Fuck, she's small. Her legs, like the rest of her, are short but nicely shaped, with narrow ankles, strong calves and thick thighs. Her hips are wide, tapering into a small waist. She looks like one of those waifs in old paintings, with a body considered the epitome of seduction in those days. Apparently it works for me, since I can barely hold back from sliding myself inside her. Trailing my hand down between her breasts, I cup one of the small globes in my palm, while bending down to play with the pebbled nipple of the other with my lips and tongue.

"Perfect," I mumble against her skin, feeling her arch off the mattress when I suck her breast in my mouth.

Isla's small hands grow impatient against my head as I change sides, before running my open mouth down her soft stomach, nipping at the pliant skin with my teeth. Her groan, and the scent of her heat, has me slide my hands behind her legs, pulling them up over my shoulders. A taste: a quick one, because I won't be able to hold back much longer.

Groomed, but not shaved, her pussy is slick with her juices, prettily swollen, and ready for my tongue.

"Sweet Pixie," I moan, when I've licked the length of her slit, back to front. Her heels dig into my back as her hips lift off the bed, eager for more.

"Please, Ben..."

Knowing I won't last long once I'm inside her, I focus on getting her taken care of first. I tease her clit with my tongue, while sliding a single digit into her tight channel. A second finger joins the first, and I feel her slowly stretch around me. I am not a small man, but I soon have her grinding herself on my hand.

"So close—I need..."

I can't ignore the sharp tugs on my hair or the whispered pleas. In a swift move I have her flipped over on her stomach, her hips pulled up, chest to the mattress and her luscious ass sticking up in the air. I have to squeeze my cock to slow down before I come all over her. Leaning over, I pull my wallet from my jeans. In seconds, I've rolled on the condom and have my cock teasing her center. With a hand braced on her hip, I ease in, struggling not to go too fast. Her cunt is like a tight fist around me. When she moans softly, clenching her fists in the sheets, I stop moving. Her head promptly shoots up and she squints at me over her shoulder.

"Don't you dare fucking stop," she spits at me. If I hadn't just been given the green light, I would have laughed at her flash of temper. To tease, I move my hips back slowly, listening to her whimper before I slam home, balls slapping against the back of her thighs. The sight of my slicked up cock disappearing into her body rips any remaining control from my grip, and my hips piston into her with muscle-burning force.

"Fuuck, baby," I grunt, curving myself around her back when I feel my balls draw in tight. My hand slips around and between her legs, where I'm surprised to find her own fingers already working frantically. Covering her hand with mine, I add pressure to the friction, and I soon feel her come with a full body shudder I can feel massaging my cock. With my arm wrapped around her chest, I pull her with me when I rise up on my haunches. Her back tight to my front, and my arm keeping her anchored, I furiously drive up into her, finally grunting my own release in her neck.

I drop sideways on the bed, my arm still holding her tight and my cock still connecting us. *I'm gonna feel that tomorrow.* It takes more than just a few minutes to catch my breath. Reluctantly, I carefully pull out, quickly taking care of the condom in the bathroom.

She hasn't moved an inch when I carefully crawl in behind her, thinking she's fallen asleep until I hear her soft voice.

"Can we do that again?"

I bury my face in the back of her neck and laugh. Fucking forty-eight years old, without a decent sleep in days; not to mention I almost gave myself a heart attack just now—and still she manages to make me feel like a fucking teenage horn dog.

CHAPTER 7

He sleeps like the dead.

I've been watching him for the past twenty minutes since I woke up. His full lips slightly parted on the soft snores filling my bedroom. My eyes have traced every exposed part of him there is to see, from the firm, wide chest under the dense mat of silver hair, to the straight line of his slightly flared nose. The permanent set of creases between his eyebrows is barely softened with sleep and seems harsh against his relaxed features. I know nothing about the man and yet, more than once already, he's jumped in the fray for me.

I know he rides a bike, has a truck, is, according to him, semi-retired, although from what I have no idea. I also know he carries a gun, as became apparent last night, something that's been plaguing me since. I know it's not uncommon to carry a concealed weapon, especially in these parts, but it's always been something I've felt uncomfortable around. My eyes involuntarily drift back to the weapon; he so carelessly tossed on the bedside table earlier, before shifting back to him. Unable to hold back any longer, my fingers reach out and revel in the feel of his skin. Soft but tough.

"Mmmm..." he mumbles in his sleep, turning his head away from me. As my fingers slide softly up along the strong lines of his neck, they encounter a ridge just at the base of his beard. I lean in a bit closer and see the puckered skin of a scar, just this side of his Adam's apple.

I lightly touch it with the pad of my index finger, when the steel band of his hand catches my wrist. My eyes shoot up to meet his ice blue ones, peeking at me from under heavy lids.

"Don't," he says, his voice almost nonexistent.

"Why?" I want to know, my finger still tracing the scar, despite the tightening of his hand around me. "What happened to you? Were you sick? Is that why your voice is always raspy?"

With a firm tug, he removes my hand and almost jumps out of bed, disappearing into the bathroom. I roll on my back and stare at the ceiling, ignoring him when I hear the toilet flush and feel the mattress dip under his weight.

"Hey." His face appears in my view and looks almost contrite. With his big palm, he strokes some stray hair off my face. "Sorry," he says on a slight tilt of his lips. "I don't like talking about it."

Feeling a little guilty for prying, I lift my hand to his face and rest it along his jaw. "I shouldn't have pried."

"You didn't pry. I...I got injured at work. It damaged my voice box, and now I sound like a walking advertisement for a horror movie."

I can't help the giggle bubbling up. It's funny and actually very true; he does sound like he could be the lead in a creepy movie. I'm glad he meant it as the joke for which I took it, judging by the gleam of humor in his eyes. My second hand joins the first to brace his face, and I pull him toward me.

"I think it's sexy," I confess, when his nose touches mine.

"Yeah?" he rasps.

"Uh-huh." I nod, rubbing the tip of my nose along his and seeking out his lips with mine.

The kiss is soft, sweet, all the more so because his crystal clear eyes stay focused on mine the entire time. I try to suppress the butterflies starting to swarm inside my chest, but I'm afraid it's already too late.

Since neither of us bothered getting dressed earlier, there's no delay in getting as close as two bodies can possibly be. Which we accomplish in very short order, Ben buried deep inside me, this time with his unexpectedly soft eyes on my face instead of my ass. The languid pace of our morning loving brings on a much less volatile, but no less soul shattering orgasm than the one he gave me during the night. I have to admit; either way works for me.

It's close to nine o'clock by the time I surface from my postcoital daze to find Ben standing beside the bed, tucking his gun in the small of his back. I'd forgotten all about it.

"What is it that you do...exactly?" I want to know. "Government employee you said?"

"Different things," he evades without any apparent shame in doing so. "I'm sent off on different projects." Before I have a chance to push him for more than that vague explanation, he presses a hard kiss to my lips. "I've gotta run," he states. "Got a meeting I'm gonna be late for."

Without a chance to ask for clarification, I watch his very nice ass disappear through the door. So many questions, so few answers.

I moan as I drag my ass out of bed and into the shower, feeling every little bit of last night's, as well as this morning's, activities down to my toes. With Ben off doing God knows what, I think I'll head to Cortez, get those images printed, and drop them off at the bakery in town after.

Funny, how opportunities open up for you the moment you decide to open up to them. In more than one way. I've done some really cool edits on the five shots I selected and am hoping I can find some decent frames for them. That way if Jen, the owner of The Pony Express, likes them, they're ready to go up on the wall. Perhaps a little too optimistic, but it doesn't hurt to have a positive outlook.

Deciding on a bit more put-together look today, I pull my one and only summer dress from the one tiny wardrobe this trailer boasts. It's dressier than I'd normally be comfortable in, but I find with my feet in rubber flip-flops, I don't feel completely out of my zone. They actually look quite cute, the red matching the color of the large poppies covering the retro fifties sundress I pulled off the rack in a thrift store. The shoulder straps aren't too wide, the bodice fits me like a glove, and the skirt is wide and flirty: very girly, but with my boyish haircut and selection of footwear, it isn't froufrou.

-

The printer where I order the photos needs only two hours, so I grab a quick bite for lunch at a small diner on Main Street and capitalize on the fact that my cell phone finally has a few bars showing by calling my uncle. Ginnie is doing a little better. Apparently, during a lucid moment, she's now agreed to move into the full-time care facility Uncle Al had found for her. He, on the other hand, is struggling with guilt and understandable sadness. After not only having to say goodbye to his sister and the love of his life, he also is preparing to say goodbye to the woman he's shared the past eighteen or so years with. I understand the sadness and also the loneliness that will undoubtedly follow after she's gone.

That kind of loneliness settles in your bones until it just becomes part of who you are. Not wanting to be an island in a sea of people, trying constantly to find that right connection, but ending up one just the same.

I manage to cheer him up some when I tell him all is running smoothly on the mountain, not wanting to worry him with things he can't do anything about anyway. His mood is considerably better when I finally end the call. After paying for my lunch and leaving a tip on my table, I head back to my car.

I hit up two places for frames to fit the 20" by 30" prints I've ordered, walking away with five unique pewter colored frames. All different, but still looking like a set because of the metallic sheen. Initially the size made me a little nervous, but the guy at the lab assured me that the quality of the shots could handle it. That had made me feel really fricking good and the day's only gotten better since. By the time I'm heading back to Dolores, the pictures beautifully framed with the help of the dude at Southwest Printing, I'm really excited.

When I leave The Pony Express an hour after that, my prints safely tucked inside Jen's office, waiting to be added to her gallery wall after the weekend, I'm positively over the moon. Rushing up the mountain, I'm eager to get started editing some of my other shots.

I pull into my parking spot at the back of the trailer and glance over at Ben's trailer below. I'm surprised to find the bike in its usual spot, but the pickup truck gone. I've only ever seen him on his bike. My mind occupied with thoughts on what he might be up to, I don't notice the curtains on the bedroom window shifting slightly.

"Look," I tell Luis the moment I arrive. "You fucking hired me for security. To make sure to keep people away from this side. I don't mind picking up a few supplies, but I'll be damned if I drive all the fucking way to Moab to make a delivery for you. Get him to do it." I point my thumb over my shoulder, where I know Carlos is listening closely.

A ping on the satellite phone Luis had supplied me with alerted me to a message, just as I got to my trailer this morning. His text had simply said: *10 mins—Moab—shipment*. I'd used the ten minutes to put on fresh clothes before making my way over to the far side of the campground.

I don't like the look on his face as Luis stares me down. "Think carefully," he says, his voice low with threat. "I appear to be short a courier and a very important customer is impatient. Carlos is needed here. Consider thoroughly before you question your duties—or I will have to question them for you."

I wasn't about to show him my excitement. This was the turn in the case we'd been waiting for, an opportunity to take down not only the meth lab, but also hopefully the distribution network. My resistance was only for Luis' benefit. The guy he thinks I am wouldn't easily be pushed around, so I could hardly pump my fist and do a happy dance. I had to stick to my role.

That's why I took my time to end the stare down, finally just shifting my eyes to the side and grunting my yield on the matter. The firm clap of his hand on my shoulder confirmed I'd played my cards right. A man like Luis would have no respect for someone weak. That could get me dead.

Once he and Carlos help me load up, closing the cover on my truck bed tightly, I head out. I hate seeing Isla's trailer get smaller in my rearview mirror, but the sooner I put another nail in the local drug trade's coffin, the closer I'll be to wrapping things up. Isla will be safe, and I'll have plenty of time to think of her and of my future. The one I'm starting to see my Pixie part of.

-

"You've got a tail."

I just passed through Dove Creek and am about ten minutes from the Utah border when the warning comes through my earpiece. Immediately my eyes fly to my rearview mirror but I don't see much.

"How the fuck can you tell I have a tail?" Been driving this damn highway north for the past hour without stopping, so how anyone can make a tail in the steady stream of traffic heading north, I don't know. The chuckle from the FBI agent on the other side grates like nails on a chalkboard, but I bite my tongue, well aware that he's part of the team I'm trusting to have my back on this. In this case, a team that is setting up in position at the address of the warehouse in Moab I'd been given.

"It's the silver Tahoe," he clarifies, sending a chill down my spine. Something is going down.

"Got a bead on the driver?" Descriptions for the trailer, the vehicle, and the two men have long been part of the file.

"Carlos." Is his answer. "Makes no sense, he's not getting closer, we're just passing the motel in Dove Creek."

I'd have to agree. It doesn't make any sense to me either, unless they are testing me. Figure we'll soon find out.

By the time I pull into the open loading dock of the warehouse in Moab, I've guessed and second-guessed Luis' motivations for sending Carlos after me. I don't have to wait long, because the familiar silver SUV pulls in right behind me. I stay in my seat as instructed and in my side mirror watch Carlos get out and walk up to my driver's side. I slowly lower my window, slipping into my role as muscle for hire.

"This is fucked, Carlos. What's the deal here?"

The younger man just shrugs his shoulders. "Bossman says I gotta keep an eye on you. I'm keeping an eye on you. That's all."

"This a test? Cause if it is, it doesn't make any sense to me. Easier just to send you." I unbuckle and open the car door, pushing Carlos out of the way. I don't want to have to make a move before the buyer gets here, but I'm ready if I have no choice.

"How else are we gonna know you can be trusted, amigo?"

I give him a dirty look before moving to the back of the truck, where I unlock and open the cover. A door in the back opens and three men walk in. A short guy in a suit, in the middle, holding a briefcase and two more casually dressed goons by his side. I pretend to ignore them and start unloading the truck, while Carlos walks up to meet them. Together they head this way, yapping in Spanish the entire way.

I step back from the containers I've stacked on the fold out table against the wall. One of the three guys walks over and starts opening random lids, checking the contents with a field scanner. Those things don't come cheap, at about five grand a pop, so I assume this is a serious operation. I lean against the side of my truck, just steps away from the driver's side door, trying to look casual while still keeping an eye on everyone around me.

The moment the guy in the suit drops the case on the table and opens it, stacks of money visible, the loading dock is suddenly teeming with agents. I barely have a chance to draw my weapon at the first sound of shots fired, when it's over. One of the goons is on the ground, bleeding from his arm, by the looks of it, and the others are all facing the agents in front of them.

All except Carlos, his eyes are burning into mine, and with a small smile on his mouth, he mumbles something under his breath. Sounds like *cheap shot?*

CHAPTER 8

"I see I'm not the only one who's been looking." The voice from behind me sends shivers down my spine when I enter the trailer, walking straight to the kitchen to drop my take out coffee and my purse. Whatever I'm holding in my hands falls to the floor as I whirl around, finding the shower creep standing in the passage to my bedroom. My eyes instantly slide to the door, trying to gauge whether I could get there before him.

"Don't bother trying," he says, as if reading my thoughts.

I back up to the counter as he slowly moves toward me, my hands behind me, hoping I can reach the knife block beside the stove.

"Nuh-huh." He wags his finger in front of his face, while his other hand comes up holding a gun he points directly at me. "We have some unfinished business, you and I, no? I told you how much I enjoyed seeing you on your knees. Imagined fucking that mouth of yours. Seeing my *ese* walk out of here this morning pissed me off. Knowing you were giving it to the *conjo*."

I can't control the hammering of my heart in my chest, but when he talks about Ben, his *ese,* leaving my trailer this morning, the blood freezes in my veins. Even with my limited Spanish, I know that means brother. *That* means this revolting man is more than just a fellow camper, and Ben has obviously not been straight with me.

"Ahhh, I see this is a surprise?" His face twists into a sneer. "Your boyfriend has not told you. This pleases me."

I'm confused and terrified, as violent shaking takes over my body. Something the man takes immediate advantage of as he clears the distance in two steps. I find myself with my back plastered against his front, one arm around my waist and the other pressing the gun against the side of my neck. In a brief flash, I see the scar on Ben's neck, and I know instinctively this is how he got his.

Pressing every disgusting inch of him against me, he pushes me toward the coffee table, where my camera was sitting right on top of the printouts I made earlier in the week.

"Imagine my surprise to find these while I was waiting," he hisses in my ear. "Spying on us the whole time, were you?"

I frantically shake my head. "No...No, I wasn't. It was an accident. I was just—"

I never get to finish my sentence, because I find myself thrown to the side, my head catching the edge of the kitchen table before my world turns black.

It's closing on three in the afternoon when I pull into the parking lot at The Pony Express to meet with the rest of my team. I've been in telephone contact with them the entire time, strategizing the best way to take down an armed felon, who is holed up in a highly explosive meth lab in the middle of the day. I've made it here in less than an hour and a half, leaving the warehouse in the capable hands of the FBI as I rushed back.

I barely sit down with my team when a woman with a large framed print in her hands walks out from behind the counter, holding it up against the far wall, obviously trying to pick a spot. When I see the actual image, I'm up out of my chair like a flash, a sick feeling heavy in my gut.

"Excuse me. Is that Isla Ferris' work?" I ask the surprised woman. The image is of a cow, the early morning sun reflecting of the water creating a halo around its head. In the background I can clearly recognize the dock at the campground.

"Wow," the lady says with a bright smile on her face. "Now I'm really excited to hang these. Yes—

yes, it is. In fact, she just dropped them off maybe forty-five minutes ago."

I feel a bit of relief to hear Isla was here not that long ago. I nod at the woman and walk back to the table, where my three teammates are watching me curiously.

"What's with the sudden interest in snapshots?" one of them asks when I sit down. For some reason his question raises the hair on my arm. Something about Carlos' reaction had been bugging me, but I hadn't been able to put a finger on it. Realization hits like the final tumbler of a lock sliding home, making my blood run cold.

Snap shot...not *cheap shot!*

That's what the fucker said. It was a threat.

I shoot up from my chair and lean in, my hands on the table.

"He's got Isla."

"Isla? Is that the camp manager?" Joe Francisi, my boss, asks.

"Change of plans," I announce, before wasting precious minutes to outline my intent to go in alone, having the team on stand-by just north of the campground. Ignoring the loud objections behind me, I hurry out the door, jump in my truck, and race up the mountain.

I don't bother stopping at her trailer, and instead drive straight down to site forty-nine. Either he has her and expects me, or he doesn't, but he'll still be expecting me. The moment I slam the door shut, my weapon at the small of my back, I see the door of the trailer open a crack. Pretending not to notice, I do what I normally do; sit down in one of the folding chairs to the side of the door, waiting for Luis to show himself. I've never been inside the trailer, but I have a general idea of the layout. It's likely been changed somewhat to suit their purposes, but other than the pungent odor associated with *cooking,* from the outside there's little distinguishing the trailer as a meth lab.

"Everything go okay?"

I turn my head to find Luis standing with one foot on the step, half of his body still obscured by the doorframe.

"Yup," I answer easily, trying not to let my rage show. The thought of any harm coming to Isla forces me to draw on the decades of carefully honed patience and control, just to keep my seat and not rip the bastard apart. I only manage to do that because I fear what he has on the other side of that door is hanging on to life by a mere thread.

Luis turns his head to look up the road before his eyes find me again, a grin spreading on his face. "Carlos?" he says.

"Scared the shit out of me," I said, knowing I'd have to tread careful. "Not cool, Luis. Setting me up like that."

"Just needed to know if I could trust you," he shrugs unapologetically. "By the way, where is he?"

"Who, Carlos? He said something about stopping for gas. Shouldn't be far behind me."

He glances up the road one more time before pushing the door a little wider. "Toss your gun in the truck. We've got a problem," he says casually, tilting his head to invite me in. Reluctantly I pull my weapon free and toss it in the back of the pickup, following him into the trailer.

My head is throbbing when I wake up and find myself on the disgusting floor of a trailer. The head hurts either from hitting the table, or from the God-awful stench that is starting to penetrate. The next thing I notice is the sound of voices. The creep I found in my trailer is standing with one foot outside the door, but with that gun still trained in my direction. The other voice I recognize instantly and the sound causes my stomach to churn. Part of me wants to scream for help, but another, bigger, part is afraid of what will happen if I do. I don't know if I can handle having him confirm he played me all along. So I stay still and close my eyes, even when I feel the trailer move when the men obviously step inside.

"What's she doing here?" I hear Ben casually ask, and it takes everything out of me not to move at those callous words, tearing into my core.

"Saw you coming from her trailer this morning, *esé*. Went to check her trailer out; found those."

I can't see what he's pointing at, but the rustling of paper tells the story. He's showing Ben the pictures. I don't think I ever ended up actually telling him I had taken those shots.

"Your *puta* was spying on us."

"Son of a bitch," Ben's voice rasps after a brief pause. "Jesus, man. I had no idea."

Hoping both men's focus is on the pictures or each other, instead of on me, I very carefully try to sneak a peek, my eyelids still mostly closed. All I can decipher is that although Ben is facing in this direction, the other guy is standing level with my hips, his feet slightly turned away.

"The fuck, Luis?" I hear Ben call out.

That's when I spot the raised arm, aiming straight at Ben's chest. Before I can even think it through, I pull up my knees, kicking my top leg out, just as the sound of a gunshot reverberates off the walls of the trailer and chaos ensues. My ears are ringing as I watch Ben hit the floor in front of me. Hard.

More shots ring out and I wait for the one I know will mean the end for me.

CHAPTER 9

"Clear!"

I'm still trying to suck in air when I hear Joe's call. The slug hit me on the right side of my chest, knocking me clear off my feet. Getting old sucks, because I'm thinking the impact may well have cracked a few ribs.

Thank God for an unseasonably cool day, which made wearing a vest under my zip up hoodie possible.

I roll my head to look at Isla, who'd clearly been playing possum earlier, and now has her eyes squeezed tightly shut. I still can't believe she tried to intervene. Too late for the first shot, but she managed to get him off balance, which saved me from a potential second one and gave Joe and the team time to get in here. I knew they'd be right behind me, that they'd see me toss my gun and take their cue from that. They didn't disappoint; Joe took Luis down before he even set foot in the trailer.

"Pixie." I try to get her attention as I struggle to push myself up, but my voice doesn't reach. With my team crowding into the trailer, there's too much noise drowning me out. I manage to crawl on hands and knees over to where Joe is crouching beside her. "Move," I grunt at his back. He shifts slightly, and finally I see those beautiful hazel eyes on me. Relief shows first, but then weariness clouds them.

"Who the hell are you?" Her voice sounds rough, almost as rough as mine.

"DEA," Joe answers for me and I throw him a glare.

By the time my eyes get back to Isla, hers are firmly closed again, shutting me, or perhaps this entire scene, out. It doesn't stop me from trailing my fingers over her face.

"Barnes," Joe calls one of my teammates. "Help Gustafson on his feet and get him outside. Right behind you with the girl."

"Bullshit. I'm taking her," I growl at him, before getting my legs under me. Gritting my teeth I manage to get my arms under her and lift her up. "Come on, Pixie. Let's get you out of here."

She doesn't struggle or even object as I carry her outside, but I can feel the distance in her. Barnes is right behind me, and drags one of the folding chairs over to the picnic table.

"Sit her down here," he says. Barnes is the resident medic on our team, which comes in handy from time to time. I step back and let him do his thing, while I take off my hoodie and my shirt, loosening the Velcro straps at my side. It hurts like a son of a bitch when I lift the vest over my head. A sharp hiss escapes my lips and Isla whips her head around, her eyes growing big as she takes me in.

"He got you good," Barnes observes, checking out the already growing deep purple bruise. "You probably need to get those ribs taped up."

I don't get a chance. Next thing I know Joe whisks me away to talk to local law enforcement, who've just arrived on the scene.

-

"What the fuck do you mean, she's being transported to Flagstaff?"

With local and federal law enforcement now swarming the campground, I'd lost complete track of Isla. Last I knew, Barnes was driving her to the medical center in Dolores to get her seen by a doctor. Aside from the knock on her head, she didn't seem to be hurt anywhere else, thank God, but better to make sure.

That had been hours ago.

Now, with the scene somewhat under control after we'd evacuated the rest of the sites, I finally had a minute to check on her.

"Just that," Joe replies sardonically. "When she found out the camp would have to be shut down, while we deal with the lab and dive the reservoir, she said that's where she wanted to go."

"Fuck!" I swing around and hurl the coffee someone handed me earlier at a tree.

"Word of advice," Joe says behind me. "Not sure what went on with her, but I'm thinking she could use some time to catch her breath. In the meantime, you should consider getting this case sorted and your retirement finalized. Get your own head straight before you chase after her."

I stalk away without saying anything, but Joe's words follow me all the way to my trailer. I'm pissed things went down like this, that I didn't have a chance to explain things to that waif of a woman, who has clouded my brain and twisted my insides with just a few tastes of her spirit. Not enough. Not nearly enough.

For years, I'd been biding my time until I could walk away from this life of constant subterfuge. From a role that forced me to rub shoulders and make nice with the literal scum of the earth. I feel caked with the filth I've rolled around in for the past decades, and I know Joe is right. I need time to scrape it off before I pollute anyone else's life. Something I didn't care about before.

I care now, thinking about that wide, unbridled smile, the sharp little tongue and those gorgeous hazel eyes that are unable to hide the depth of emotion inside.

-

"This Gustafson?" The gruff voice on the other side barks when I answer my phone.

"It is."

"Al Ferris here. Need to have a word."

I don't even bother asking how he got my number; Isla's uncle still likely has his connections. I also don't bother asking why he's calling because I know the answer to that, as well.

"I figured," I simply say, which launches Al into an expected tirade about putting his niece in danger. I let him rant until he slows down before I react.

"I like her," is what I open with, and from the silence on the other side of the line, I gather he wasn't expecting that. "I had no intention of involving her until I caught her snooping around." I continue to explain, as calmly as I can, the sequence of events, which thankfully the man allows me to do without interruption. After I've given him the story, a heavy silence hangs in the air.

"You like her?" he finally repeats.

"That's what you're left with?" I question him, chuckling.

"Well, fuck yeah...Since the girl I've seen grow up, always with a smile, now has to struggle to slap one on. Nothing brings her down. Nothing. Not since she was a teenager. She won't let it."

By the time Al ends the call, I haven't only been ripped a new one and made to promise to set thing right with her, I have a deeper understanding of the deep-rooted pain that's never quite hidden behind Isla's broad smiles.

CHAPTER 10

"Hey, Isla. Are those the new ones?"

Jen comes rushing from behind the counter, her eyes on the large tote in my hand. I was absolutely floored when she called two weeks ago to tell me all five of my prints were sold. I'd still been in Flagstaff, spending some quality time with my uncle and Ginnie, before she was moved into her new 'home.'

Uncle Al had initially been adamant he didn't want me to go back to Dolores. Especially, when I mentioned I'd gotten acquainted with Ben. He appeared to pick up on what I purposely left out, judging by the squint of his eyes.

"Should never have left you there by yourself," he'd muttered angrily, before disappearing into his office, where I heard him have a spirited conversation over the phone. My guess is he got the nitty gritty of what happened from one of his old police contacts, because when he finally resurfaced, his mood was better. Not good, but better.

By the time DEA Special Agent Francisi called to let me know they'd have the campground cleared in a day or two, my uncle hadn't balked much at all when I announced I'd be heading back the next day. I have to admit, I was a bit freaked to find out they'd fished the remains of a well-known local drug peddler from the depths of the reservoir. Apparently that was the garbage I'd seen the other man toss overboard. I didn't even want to think what it meant that it apparently had taken several bags to dispose of the body.

I did ask about Ben. I'd already surmised in the chaos after the shots rang out, he was some kind of cop. It was a relief to find out he wasn't some vile drug dealer, but it didn't change the deep sense of betrayal I felt. Mostly though, I was angry at myself, for apparently not having learned enough in my life to keep my heart safe. After losing the two most important people in my life at a young age, I'd known I wouldn't be able to handle going through that kind of profound loss again. Just the prospect of one day losing Uncle Al, as well, was enough to avoid allowing room in my heart for anyone else. Judging by the persistent ache in my chest, I didn't do such a bang up job. In the short time we'd know each other, I'd somehow let Ben in only to discover it was never about me. He'd played his role well. So well, that he left a hole.

"He's fine," Joe told me. "Will be signing his final papers next week and he'll be on his way."

Good. That meant there was no risk of running into him. I was packed and ready to go the next day.

"Yes, they are." I smile when Jen takes the bag from my hand and starts pulling out the frames.

"Oh my goodness," she whispers. "These are exquisite."

The shots are ones I took that night on the dock. One shows a hint of the mountains reflected in the surface off the water, with the huge expanse of the star-streaked night sky above. That's the one Jen is holding up.

"How did you manage this?" She points at the light streaks.

"Slow shutter speed," I hear a voice behind me, and my heart lodges in my throat. "Isn't that what you told me, Pixie?" he says softly in my ear.

I fight the urge to turn around, just as I fight the blasted tears flooding and subsequently escaping my eyes. *Damn him!* I try to focus on Jen, who looks stunned as she flicks her eyes from my now tear-stained face, over my shoulder, where I can feel Ben looming close. The heat from his body is pulling at me, and I curse myself for being too weak to ignore him. As much as I know I'm just handing him more ammunition to hurt me, there's part of me that wants to hear what he has to say.

"Excuse me," Jen mutters, a little flustered. "I have...I mean, I should check...on things."

Well, this is uncomfortable.

"Ten minutes." His soft, raspy voice has a pleading quality I've not yet heard from him. "I get you're mad, but I'm asking for ten minutes of your time."

My back still turned to him; I take a deep breath in. "It was you, wasn't it?" I ask, looking at the empty spots on the wall, where I assume my prints have hung. He knows exactly what I'm talking about and answers instantly.

"Needed a piece of you. Something to remind me that through your eyes, there's beauty everywhere. That getting to know you allowed me a glimpse too, even if all I've seen for years is an ugly world."

I literally can feel the fissure in my heart crack wider at his words, and I can't help the sliver of hope that fills it.

"Please." His breath whispers over the shell of my ear and has me finally turn around.

I can almost feel the touch of those clear pale blue eyes as he scans my face. I recognize his regret when he sees my tears. "Pixie..."

"Okay," I manage. "But not here."

I follow her black bug up the mountain, noticing her occasional glances in the rearview mirror to ensure I'm still there. *I'm not going anywhere, baby.*

A month since I last saw her. Four weeks: I've spent writing reports, wrapping up my investigation for the most part, and hours upon hours of debriefing.

Twenty-eight days, in which I've made a healthy start at shedding the life I'm leaving behind, taking steps in creating a new one. Six hundred and seventy-two hours of wishing I'd been able to handle things in a way that wouldn't have caused the hurt I saw in her eyes. Forty thousand, three hundred and twenty minutes, not one of which passed without a thought of her, hoping...

I pull in beside her and cast a glance at the large family tent now occupying site forty-nine. A lot of the sites are occupied, including twenty-three. My old trailer is gone, it belonged to my old life, and I sold it without any qualms.

Isla stands a bit uncomfortably beside her car. Her tears seem to have dried up—*thank fuck*—but her unease is palpable. I put my bike on the kickstand, take off my shades, and resolutely reach for her hand. A small tug and she turns ahead of me, leading me into her trailer, not once letting go of my hand.

"I'm scared," she mumbles with her back to me when I close the door behind me.

"So am I," I admit, surprising her. She spins around with questions in her eyes. Questions she deserves answers for.

"I was in my early twenties when I started working for the DEA," I start, still holding tight to her hand. "My first investigation ended up a clusterfuck of epic proportions that ended in a standoff. One that ended with one team member dead and one injured."

"You," she says immediately.

"Me," I confirm. "It was a raid on a crack house in Denver. Four of us went in, and I was supposed to clear the kitchen. A little too anxious and overly eager, I missed the pantry door. Before I knew what was happening, someone grabbed me in a stranglehold, pressing a barrel under my chin." I notice the slight wince on her face and shake my head before I continue. "Brad was a good man. A good friend and the only family I had. After that, I took on every undercover assignment I could get my hands on. It suited me...until I got tired of the stench of wading in the constant sewage." When I pause, Isla guides me wordlessly to the couch, pulling me down beside her.

"Go on," she urges me.

"I didn't expect you. Al...well, Al being an ex-cop, I was going to fill him in on the goings on under his nose. Although I'm pretty sure he had his suspicions already: about site forty-nine and about me. I had it all under control...up till you complimented my bike and smiled like you'd just won the lottery, despite the pain that was clear in your eyes." She immediately lowers her eyes to hide what I've seen there from the start. "Roped into this investigation at the last minute, I just wanted to see it through, so I could finally walk away. Be done." My voice is getting rougher with every sentence, but I'm determined to finish. Then it'll be up to her. "Isla—look at me." With a finger under her chin, I tilt her head up. "What ended up happening between us had *nothing* to do with the job, and everything to do with person you are—regardless of how it started."

"I know," she whispers, surprising me. "I was using it as an excuse to walk away."

"Why?" I ask, though I have a good idea already.

"Afraid," she echoes what she said earlier, shrugging her shoulders slightly and dropping her head down. "Of how deep you had rooted inside me, in such a short time. It meant that by the time you'd decide to walk away, the damage would be even bigger." Her eyes find mine and I squeeze her hand in encouragement. "My mom...she..."

"I talked to Al," I interrupt her, the pain in her voice cutting me. "He contacted me a few weeks ago. Tore a strip off me first." I chuckle at the memory of the old man, threatening to tear off my balls and shove them down my throat. He was dead serious at the time, too. "He told me about your mom and your aunt." I clear my throat as I cup her jaw in my hand and tilt her head up. "I get it."

The last is no more than a whisper as I close my mouth over hers. Tentative at first—testing her—but when her lips open, inviting my tongue, she throws caution to the wind. Throwing her leg over mine, so she is straddling my lap, she gives herself with no reservation. Her fingers twisted in my hair, and the other hand pressed against my chest, she shows me exactly what's in her heart. I'm fucking elated.

By the time I have her divested of her clothes and am buck-naked myself, we're both breathing hard. I lift her up off the couch, where she'd ended up underneath me while our hands and mouths explored and tasted, and carry her to the bed, climbing in with her body clutched to mine.

"Hurry, Ben," she tries to rush me, fingers clawing at my skin and her legs opening wide in invitation.

"Shhh...easy, baby," I say, dropping my hips between hers. "Look at me." When I have her beautiful eyes on me, I slowly enter her body, the look of bliss on her face reflecting my emotions.

Nothing is held back as I try to show her with my body what may be too soon to tell her. When I finally see her eyes glaze over, and feel her body clamp down on mine, I let go, throwing my head back as I come hard, grunting her name.

"Ben?" Isla's voice sounds muffled against my chest a little later. I've rolled us so I'm on my back, and she's draped on top as we catch our breath.

"Mmmm..."

"What happens now?"

"Whatever we want, Pixie," I answer, idly stroking circles on the soft skin of her ass. "We don't need rules, we can just make it up as we go."

She lifts up her face and looks me in the eye, her hand coming up to touch my face.

"I think I'm falling," she says with a soft smile. I turn my head and kiss her palm, keeping my eyes on her.

"Baby...I've already landed."

THE END

Read more about Ben and Isla in the full sized novel
"FREEZE Frame"

coming Spring 2017

Keep reading for an excerpt!!

FREEZE FRAME

By
Freya Barker & K.T. Dove

(unedited excerpt)

CHAPTER I

Isla

"Mmmm..."

Ben groans as he rolls over on his back the moment I slip my arm from around his waist.

The soft light of an early sun is coming through the small window opposite the bed, as I untangle myself from the sheets and slip into the bathroom to relieve myself.

He's still softly snoring when I get back. A quick peek at the clock, on the nightstand, shows only six in the morning. To get up or crawl back under the covers, that is the question. After reacquainting myself with all Ben is able to do to my body last night—making up for lost time—I could probably do with another hour, maybe two. I'm still tired, and not just a little sore from last night's thorough workout.

Ben's face is lined with deep grooves, mapping out the hard life he's led. Every line a witness to the decade or more he's spent working undercover for the DEA, living side by side with some of the most depraved and vile criminals. It marks a man. It's marked Ben, but every line and every wrinkle he wears just adds to his appeal. His heavily fringed eyelids fan across his cheeks, his full lips slack with sleep.

Beauty in contrast. Something I have an eye for, being a photographer. Everything about Ben is both soft and hard; it wasn't hard to fall for him.

I slide back underneath the sheets and my body automatically seeks his warmth, curling up against his side.

"Mmmmm, babe…" he mumbles sleepily, curving his arm around me and tugging me closer. "It's early."

"I know. Go back to sleep," I whisper.

I try practicing what I preach. My eyes drift shut, but the soft circular strokes of Ben's calloused fingertips on my neck at the hairline, keep me from drifting off. My skin is sensitized to the point that I almost anticipate the path of his touch. When his fingers change course and brush along my spine, all the way down to my ass, my skin buzzes with electricity and all hope of sleep disappears.

"You're not sleeping," I mutter, only slightly accusingly into his chest, as I trail my fingers through the hair there. His chuckle rumbles under my ear.

"Neither are you," he says, his big hand sliding down to cup my ass. Well, half of my ass, seeing as even his shovel-sized paws can't cover all my real estate.

"Mmmm, you sure you can manage after last night, old man?" His hand squeezes as he rolls me on top of him. My knees drop on either side of his hips and it is immediately evident how well he'll be able to manage. No words are needed, his solid erection rubbing along my slick core is plenty of proof.

"Isla," he growls, his hands settling firmly on my hips, holding me in place. "We have to talk."

Ignoring him, I lean forward, nipping his full bottom lip with my teeth,

"Later," I mumble against his mouth before sliding my tongue inside.

One of his hands slips back over my ass, while the other comes up to cup the back of my head. In one move, he sits up on his knees and has me on my back, my legs draped wide over his thighs. I shiver when his hand slips around to the front where he leaves it curved around my neck, the light pressure keeping me still as he bends forward and takes my nipple between his lips. The light bite followed by the wet heat of his mouth, has my hips lift up, eager for friction.

"Easy," he whispers against my skin. "Lift your arms over your head and keep them there." I don't question him and do as he tells me. Not because I don't have a mind of my own, but because he's already proved to me that he knows better than I do how to make me feel good. My expertise is mostly reserved to the number of settings on my vibrator. Any sex with another person involved was long ago and barely memorable.

Ben is memorable. Has been since the first time we slept together a couple of months ago. My body had been played to perfection, much like he is making it sing now. Both of his palms are scraping slowly over my sensitized nipples, dragging down over the soft swell of my stomach to the junction of my thighs. His thumbs play lazily through the wet gathering there, brushing lightly through my folds. His eyes are focused on his hands—on my body—before he lifts them up to mine.

"Pretty." Is all he says before he grabs me by the hips, lifts, and with forceful precision, fills me in one powerful stroke.

My body arches off the mattress, my mouth falling open in a long drawn out groan. "Oh…"

"Eyes open." His gruffly voiced order penetrates my mindless state. I'm not even aware I have them closed. Blinking, I clear my vision, focusing on Ben's large form moving between my legs.

-

"Are you done in there?" Ben asks when I step out of the tiny bathroom, a towel wrapped around me. It would've been nice to take a shower together, but there's no way; Ben can barely fit by himself.

"Have at it." I step aside when he squeezes past me, dropping a kiss on my lips. I try hard not to giggle when I watch him work his shoulders through the door sideways, swearing under his breath. "I'll just get coffee going."

Tucking the towel in between my breasts, I step into the kitchen, thankful for the Keurig sitting on the little counter.

I'm just adding some cream and sugar to mine when the door opens behind me.

"Are you done already?" I ask, turning around with the mug already to my lips. I promptly drop my mug, spilling hot coffee all down my front. "Fuck, *ahh*!" I swing back toward the sink pulling the soaked towel away from my skin.

"Jesus, girl," my Uncle Al says, moving up behind me.

"What's wrong?" I hear behind us, as the bathroom door slams open. I turn my head in tandem with my uncle, as a buck naked Ben rushes out.

"Son of a bitch," Uncle Al bites off before he looks at me, at Ben, and marches straight back out the door. "I'll wait outside," he barks, pulling the door to the trailer shut behind him.

Wonderful.

******

Ben

"So that's how it is?" Al Ferris says when I walk outside, two coffees in hand.

"Black okay?" I hand him one, taking a deep breath before sitting down across from him at the picnic table.

I just spent ten minutes trying to calm Isla down while icing down her chest, which was burned bright red. She's getting dressed as we speak, and I don't want her to walk out here to her uncle and me going at it. So I take a sip of coffee and make sure I'm calm when I answer.

"We're together," I say simply.

"I gathered as much. For how long is what I'd like to know? Until the next assignment comes along?"

I understand his concerns. I told him as much the first time I spoke to him about his niece. It's the only reason I'm able to keep my cool.

"Al—with all due respect—I've barely had a chance to talk with Isla about the future. What I'm willing to tell you is that I care for your niece, and I have no intention to up and leave. I won't have to; I'm retired." I hold his glare until he gives his head a brisk shake and lowers his eyes.

"It complicates things," he finally says, snorting. "I came to make her an offer, but now…" His voice trails off.

"Now what?" Isla walks up and slips onto the bench beside me. "You know I can hear every word in there, right?" My hand finds her knee under the table and I give her a light squeeze.

"I forgot," Al admits, a bit contrite.

"So what brings you out here, Uncle Al? Is Ginnie okay?" The old man lifts his hand and covers Isla's.

"Ginnie is fine. Do you remember Henry Carmichael?" he asks her.

"Of course. You went to the academy together. He was at your retirement, wasn't he?"

"Yeah," Al sighs, looking down at his own fingers tracing the woodgrain in the table. I have a feeling what comes next won't be good news. "He's also the one who said that just because I was retired from the force didn't mean I should sit on my ass twiddling my thumbs." He barks out a sharp, regretful laugh. "Sitting idle would kill me, he said. This is his property, you know?"

I feel Isla startle beside me.

"His? I didn't know that."

"Yup. He bought it as an investment property when he handed in his badge a few years before me. Ran the place for a few years, and then decided a campground on a mountain wasn't gonna help him get laid."

I had to chuckle at that. I've spent enough time living from a small trailer to know that is the damn truth. Although I got lucky in the end. Al lifts his head and grins at me.

"Never got married. No kids. He was always looking for his next conquest. Damn, I swear he got worse the older he got."

The smile disappears from my face. *Was.* Which means he's dead. The small nod Al gives me is confirmation, before he lays it all out.

"I got a call last week from a lawyer in St. Petersburg, Florida, who'd been trying to reach me. Henry died from a massive heart attack, while cruising the Caribbean." This time it's Isla who reaches out and grabs her uncle's hand.

"I'm sorry," she softly says. "You've lost more than your share in this lifetime."

"Oh, baby girl—that happens when you get to be my age." The old man smiles at her. "I just prefer to think of it as being lucky I had all of them in my life: your mom, your Aunt Kate, Henry."

"Still sorry for your loss, Al," I offer my regrets, earning a hesitant smile.

"Thanks, son, but that's not why I brought Henry up." He turns his attention back to Isla, whose hand finds mine in her lap. "The lawyer who called is handling his estate. The damn bastard left me the campground. Lock, stock and barrel. Took me a bit to get my head around that. Even with Ginnie in a care facility, I don't want to be too far away. Thought about selling it." Al doesn't notice Isla going rigid beside me and forges on. "Would probably make a pretty penny, but what am I gonna do with that? My life is fine the way it is. And then there's you." He lifts his eyes to Isla. "Anyway, I had the guy send the papers I was to sign to my lawyer in Cortez and went to see him yesterday." He pulls a folded document from his inside pocket and slaps it on the table. "It's up to you, baby girl, but I had him draw these up. Figured since you seem to have found your legs here, you might want a say in this."

Trembling, Isla slips her hand from mine and draws the papers towards her. My eyes slide over her bowed head to her uncle, who gives me a slight shrug before turning his attention back on his niece.

"I don't know what to say," Isla finally mutters, shoving the papers back across the table. "It's too much."

"Bullcrap," Al reacts instantly. "It's not enough. Trust me on that. You've made my life rich, baby girl. Richer and more fulfilled than I could ever have dreamed of. You're as much mine as you were my sister's. My blood. My *only* blood. And don't think for a second you haven't brought color to Kate and Ginnie's lives, too." He sniffs loudly before letting out a hoarse chuckle. "Besides, you'll be the one doing all the work. We may both hold ownership, but you're driving the bus. That is, if you want it?"

COMING SPRING 2017

ABOUT THE AUTHOR

Freya Barker inspires with her stories about 'real' people, perhaps less than perfect, each struggling to find their own slice of happy. She is the author of the Cedar Tree Series and the Portland, ME, novels.

Freya is the recipient of the RomCon "Reader's Choice" Award for best first book, "Slim To None," and is a finalist for the 2016 Kindle Book Awards for "From Dust". She currently has two complete series and three anthologies published, and is working on two new series; La Plata County FBI—ROCK POINT, and Northern Lights. She continues to spin story after story with an endless supply of bruised and dented characters, vying for attention!

Stay in touch!

https://www.freyabarker.com
https://www.goodreads.com/FreyaBarker
https://www.facebook.com/FreyaBarkerWrites
https://twitter.com/freya_barker

or sign up for my newsletter:
http://bit.ly/1DmiBub

ACKNOWLEDGEMENTS:

Thank you to Karen Hrdlicka first and foremost for her awesome editing services.

I also owe much to Joanne Thompson for her unbelievably sharp eye, something invaluable for a proofreader and beta reader.

I have a phenomenal support group, some of whom beta and critique, while others pimp and promote! Their feedback and encouragement is something I've come to rely on so much.

I am so grateful to have my assistant Natalie Weston in my life. She finds a way to lift my spirit when I need it every time. She manages my mood swings with her unrelenting optimistic nature. She keeps me teetering on the right side of sane, and she does all this while also organizing me.

I can't forget my agent, Stephanie Delamater Phillips, whose faith in me is a constant motivator and confidence booster.

All the amazing bloggers who continue to support my books, I bow to you. You have my ongoing respect and gratitude for all you do.

And most importantly, to you, my wonderful readers. Your words of appreciation and encouragement mean the world to me.

ALSO BY FREYA BARKER

CEDAR TREE Series

Book #1
SLIM TO NONE

Book #2
HUNDRED TO ONE

Book #3
AGAINST ME

Book #4
CLEAN LINES

Book #5
UPPER HAND

Book #6
LIKE ARROWS

Book #7
HEAD START

PORTLAND, ME, Novels

Book #1
FROM DUST

Book #2
CRUEL WATER

Book #3
THROUGH FIRE

Book #4
STILL WATER

Printed in Dunstable, United Kingdom